HIS LIFE OUR STORY

"I FORGOT TO HOLD ONTO ME WHILE HOLDING ONTO HIM"

By: Totisha L. Phelps

Edited by Latasha Drax

DEDICATION

This book is dedicated to my children. I love you both more than words could ever describe. Both of you hold a special place in my heart and have played a major role in my healing process. You loved me through my struggles, and I thank both of you for allowing me to feel like the best mother in the world even when I fell short. Thank you for never giving up on me. I love y'all!

To my son from another mother, it is my prayer that this book gives you clarity while opening your heart to forgive me. No matter what, I have always loved you and always will!

To my fellow prison wives, girlfriends, and supporters, this book is also dedicated to you. Experiencing life after prison gave me a vast understanding about mental health and my goal is to raise awareness of how it affects our lives. Please take it seriously because your mental health is real and so are you!

Always Thinking of You,

Totisha,
Their Mother and Your Friend

ACKNOWLEDGEMENTS

First and foremost, I want to give honor to God for keeping me during the hardest time of my life. To my Husband, you are truly the last of the dying breed. I have watched you conquer every obstacle you have ever encountered and still stand strong. You are my best friend and I thank you for your continuous hard work, unconditional love, loyalty, and devotion to our union. We both experienced times when we wanted to give up and walk away, yet we didn't. I thank you for doing the work and I thank God for helping us to live past those moments. Thank you, Husband, for being who you are!

Always and Forever,

Your Wife,
Totisha

Dear Reader,

Although this book was designed for women involved with a man in prison or those living with a felon, everybody can learn something. So, clear your thoughts and read this book with an open mind.

Think about it for a second...we have all been in love a time or two before. This can be a love that includes people, places, or things. But how much love is too much love before you lose yourself? Let me expound briefly to give you a broader look into what I was experiencing in my relationship. My psychological well-being was compromised, and I became somewhat mentally absent. Depression is real, so know the signs. If something or someone is bothering you or you're not feeling like yourself, journal it. If you're no good for you, you're no good for the people around you.

SELF-LOVE is the *BEST LOVE*. I had to learn the hard way, so always remember to hold onto you while holding onto him, she, them, this or that. Because you're WORTH IT!

I PROMISE

What You Should Know Before Reading

I am not perfect and I am still growing spiritually. Therefore, you may bump into a profane word or two, but don't worry because I already talked to God and got His permission to express myself freely and for you to read it. So, repeat these reading vows after me:

- I promise to read this book with an open mind.
- I promise to read this book without judgment.
- I promise to read with transparency.
- I promise to use my imagination to become a part of the story as I read.

Now you are ready,

ENJOY!

TABLE OF CONTENTS

US, WE, & OURS..12

MEMORY LANE...15

COUSIN...27

VISIT TIME..30

THE DEVIL THOUGHT HE HAD ME.............................38

THE TRANSFER...42

RE-ENTRY PROGRAM..43

FAMILY INCENTIVE PROGRAM......................................45

MY CLIENTS WERE MY FAMILY.....................................48

TRUSTING GOD..49

MY NETWORK IS MY NET WORTH...............................50

SPACE & OPPORTUNITY...52

THERE'S WORK TO BE DONE.......................................54

THE PRISON AFTERMATH BEGINS...............................56

REALITY CHECK...58

WE LOVED OUR HALFWAY HOUSE FAMILY...................60

LET THE CREDIT BEGIN...62

HALFWAY HOUSE FIRST ATTENDANT...........................64

NO MORE SNEAK'N & CREEP'N...................................65

PAROLE TIME...68

DID SOMEONE SAY WEDDING?...................................74

THE HONEYMOON...80

WHAT'S BEST FOR THE CHILD.....................................83

FOOTPRINTS 89

MONEY ISN'T EVERYTHING 91

THE TWO WEEK VACATION PASS 94

LETTER FROM OFFICER 101

NEW BEGINNINGS 103

BABY LIFE 110

GOD HAS A BIGGER PLAN 115

THE SHOP 117

PARENT VS. FRIEND 125

HOSPITAL 134

JOB AFTER JOB 141

DEATH IS NEVER EASY TO PROCESS 146

BROTHER –N-LAW 155

MONEY, MOTHER & ME 160

TAKING OFF THE BLINDFOLD 163

CLOSING ARGUMENT TO THE COURT 172

IT'S OK TO BE SELFISH 174

FINAL THOUGHT 175

THE HEALING BEGINS WITH YOU 176

SERENITY PRAYER 177

THE WORK STARTS HERE 184

ABOUT THE AUTHOR 201

PRELUDE

JUDGE: The People vs. Totisha L. Phelps

BAILIFF: The Court calls Totisha L. Phelps to take the stand. Please raise your right hand and place your left hand on the Bible. Do you swear to tell the truth, the whole truth, and nothing but the truth?

ME: I do. Your Honor, may I approach the jury, please?

JUDGE: Yes, you may.

ME: Greetings, Your Honor, Jury, and the People of the Court. Let me start by introducing myself. I am Totisha L. Phelps, I was born and raised in Northern, NJ, but currently reside in the Carolinas. I have a background in business management and entrepreneurship. I love working in community relations because it is the gift that keeps on giving. In 2008, I married my childhood sweetheart after he completed a 10-year prison sentence. Although I was not behind bars myself, I still became a prisoner.

As a woman dealing with a man with a criminal background, I have faced many obstacles rooted in misconceptions, judgments, and stereotypes. As a direct result, I even battled depression and anxiety and forgot how to love myself unconditionally in the process. Although I have since conquered my depression, from time to time, I still have a moment, but to God be the glory! Learning how to meditate and talk to the Lord has allowed me to see that this journey was not only about me but other women as well.

Your Honor, I can't help but look into the women's faces in the jury box and the oversized audience. I see women who look tired, weary, and overwhelmed. I also see how well they camouflage it hiding behind their beautiful clear diamond earrings, their long string of pearls, and expensive business suits. I can also see the different shades of people that come from different backgrounds. But your Honor, I promise you that we are more alike than we are different. We are all on a journey, and deep down, we all need to hear my words today. Your Honor, don't you see, once I understood the bigger picture of my life, my mission became clear!

Initially, I was stagnant, and I struggled with how to M.O.V.E. (MAKING-OVER VALUING EXPERIENCES), but God then gave me the T.O.O.L.S. (TAKING OVER LIFE SITUATIONS) I needed to M.O.V.E. forward and succeed. I soon was able to see how to approach the mission that I was destined to do. After God yielded me to "BE STILL," I received the message that the battle was not mine anymore.

Undeniably, it was then that I knew I was chosen to deliver a message to women like me. I was on a mission to give these women a voice that will raise awareness of mental health. To help the people not like me (us) to see that the heart knows no prejudice. We love whom we love, and love conquers all. Don't you agree? The biggest obstacle I had to overcome on this journey was to be committed to myself first. I started to speak to myself daily and say, "Don't forget to hold onto to "YOU" while holding onto him!" That was the statement that allowed me to see my strength without losing touch with my reality. Your Honor, Jury, and People of the Court, here is my testimony.

US, WE, & OURS

Life is good in the Carolinas these days, although it didn't start that way. Moving to North Carolina has grown me in ways I never thought I could grow. For me, relocating to North Carolina was a spiritual move, and I didn't know it. You see, in the beginning, I didn't understand what was going on. I thought I was moving to appease my husband. But God had bigger plans for me. I say this because I had to first learn that I was sent on a mission before I understood "The US, WE, & OURS." Did y'all catch that? I had to understand the mission before I could start the process.

Life began to happen without warning. It began to rain, and I wasn't prepared for the storm. I uprooted my life, looking for a better environment for my family. However, moving to North Carolina had a significant impact on me and led to depression. Relocating came with unlimited sacrifices all at once. I left behind my hair salon business, family, and friends, on top of becoming a wife while raising my teenaged son. Not to mention, I got pregnant shortly after moving. My kids are 14 years apart! It was then my life started to get dark. The sad part is, I didn't understand what I was feeling or going through for a few years. Yes! I said it a few years.

In the beginning, I was so oblivious to what God was doing to me for the sake of us. But it is crystal clear now. Because of my faith and strength, I kept pushing until I ran out of fuel and couldn't push anymore. That was when I started to understand what I was going through. Unfortunately, I went through it alone. Not in the physical sense but mentally. I can't even explain how everything, and everyone frustrated me. But before I take it there, let me take you down memory lane.

EXHIBIT A
-WHERE WE MET-

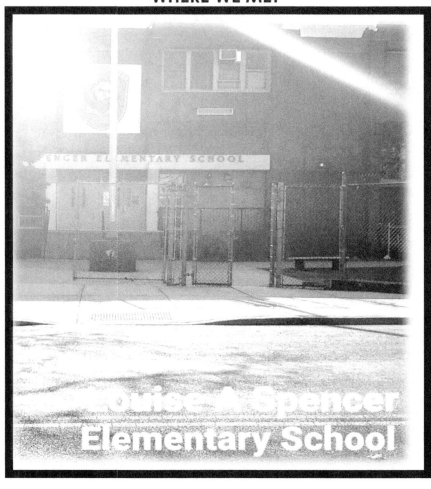

MEMORY LANE

It all started when I met my future husband on Valentine's Day in 1989. Who would have thought I would ever marry this dude? I can remember it like it was yesterday. I was in one of my favorite teacher's classes—Ms. Meredith. She taught me a lot about boys (whom she called knuckleheads), and I was at the age when girls started liking boys and vice versa. Anyway, these two boys kept coming back and forth to the classroom door making silly faces and doing all kinds of things to get my attention. One of the guys I knew and the second guy looked familiar. I didn't know who he was, but he was cute, and I was attracted to him. After watching them play in the hallway, I decided to get a hall pass to go to the bathroom. I wanted to know more about him, and we made that happen. He was a bad boy, but eventually, he became my boyfriend. We started having breakfast at my house every morning before walking to school. He would be at the back door waiting until my mother got in her car to go work. Yup! Everybody in the neighborhood was scared of my mother. He was no different. She did not play any games[1]. You know back in the day, we had structure and discipline.

---

[1] Don't tolerate nonsense

EXHIBIT B
HE WAITED HERE FOR MY MOTHER TO LEAVE

Childhood Apartment

My house was known as the party house, so everybody knew my mother's schedule and would come over. We had some good times at my house when my mother was at work and I took many beatings for the team. She kept the groceries stocked, especially during the can-can sale, which was when the supermarkets would have a blowout sale on canned goods. She also kept the house spotless or shall I say, had me slaving around the house to keep it spotless.

But it was all worth it. I knew my mother spoiled me, and so did everyone else.

I was *that* girl, and that's why he had to have me as his girlfriend. *Boyeee,* those were the good old days. I remember him coming to my house wearing his Chicago Bulls shirt and burgundy jeans. He was known for being a West Coast type of dude. He loved West Coast music and always carried a boom box-radio. He was so cool! He was different–just like me–and we understood each other.

Once we got older, we went to different high schools and sort of separated. I started meeting new boys and all of that. Although I was young and "free," he did not like the fact that I wanted to be with other boys. Me? I just wanted to have friends and have fun. But one thing about it, he was always there when I needed him. That's why, no matter what, I knew I would always have a special love for him.

EXHIBIT C
WHAT THE HOOD LOOKS LIKE TODAY

Childhood Neighborhood

WHEN I LIVED HERE, THE NOW PLAYGROUND WAS A SANDBOX FILLED WITH MONKEY BARS, A JUNGLE GYM & SLIDES

EXHIBIT D

My Mother Kept Her Promise...

Suburban Life!

When I turned 16, we moved to the suburbs. My mother always said we would be moving, but she never mentioned that it would be out of the hood[2] and away from my friends. When you're young, you're not thinking about your neighborhood being bad. You're

---

[2] Slang term for an urban neighborhood

only thinking about the good times you have with your friends. But my mother was a go-getter. She kept her word, and we got a house. Not just any house, but a mini mansion with four floors. She converted the basement for me, so I had a bedroom, living room, and a place to do hair.

Although we had a house with all these upgrades, I was not happy because it wasn't in the hood or with my friends. Also, I couldn't keep up with *him* anymore and that sucked. But no matter what, I knew he would remain relevant in my life, especially since his cousin always let me know what he was doing. Growing up, she was one of my best friends.

Eventually, I made my way back to the projects[3]. I had done everything that was asked of me by my mother. I graduated from high school and got my diploma. She wanted me to go to college, but I didn't want to. I knew how to make money, so school wasn't my priority—making money was. So, I guess you figured me out by now. One thing about me, I was always older than my time. I thought I was grown and was ready to be independent.

I started hanging out and messing with all the drug dealers. I was attracted to the money, and they had tons of it and unselfish. To be honest, I was messing with them before, but I had a curfew then, and that always put a monkey wrench in my game[4]. However, I had older cousins on my father's side of the family, and they would tell a little white lie for me if need be. The

[3] Low-income apartment in an urban community development
[4] Slang term for hustling/hustled

funniest thing, although they were older, I knew all the "ballers" and always played the matchmaker.

Anyway, one of the girls from my old neighborhood invited me to move in with her and her sister. She was one of my friends that even my mother liked, and my mother didn't trust anybody. So, I figured it was all good. I moved in and furnished my room and got a spot in a hair salon downtown. I thought I was proving my mother wrong, but after I moved out, I began to experience real-life and realized I wasn't ready to be on my own. One day, while at work, I was robbed. The thing is, I was the only one, and no one saw anything. At that point, I knew I had to play the game of the streets or go home. Since going home was not an option, I started doing me[5]. During that time, I had a strong desire to reach out to my now-husband. But I needed to be independent and couldn't allow myself to involve him. He was like me; he wore his heart on his sleeve but would also put you in your place if you overstepped your boundaries. Knowing this about him, I was smart enough to know I wasn't ready for him at that point in my life. Besides that, I knew that he was a good dude with the qualities of being a great man. So, I didn't turn to him because I didn't want to abuse him. Yet, I knew that one day I would come back prepared for him. But for now, I had to be a big girl and find my own way.

I was super smart, so getting on my feet wasn't hard; it was just exhausting. Between hustling dudes, working full-time, and partying, there was no time for

[5] Self-centered behavior to get what you need to survive

sleep. So, I continued to do me, but I always made sure he was never far out of my reach. One day I decided to go down to the projects. I had just bought a new electric blue sports car. I was the only one in the area with this Eclipse. As I pulled up into the projects, the whispers began. People started shouting that my babe had a baby with a girl he met while in high school. In the back of my mind, I was thinking Hell NO! But who was I fooling? I had a baby with someone else too. Ironically, our kids were born two weeks apart. This was a reality check that someone could steal my future husband's heart, and that was not an option. I had to seize that idea quickly and take back what was mine. I had to show back up in his world for real now and make sure I stayed relevant!

I will never forget that day. One of his cousins knew of our relationship, and she let me know he had just left the parking lot and pointed me in the direction of the street he was walking down. I sped off to try and catch him and sure enough, I saw he and his baby mother walking. I passed them at first, but then I politely put my stick shift in reverse and went to talk to "MY" man. I have always been aggressive and direct. I didn't care about her. Back then, I went for what I wanted and was out to secure mine. I had to make sure that he would love me forever, and I had to let him know that I would be around forever. So, of course, I told him I wanted to spend time with him, and we arranged to do just that. He walked his baby mother home, and I dropped my son off at his godparents. Then, I picked my Boo up from the apartment he shared with his son's mother. We left for a couple of days, and that was that. From that point on, I knew that we would be forever. We had a connection that could never be broken. Of course, we had a conversation about the nature of his relationship with his child's mother. Not that it mattered either way. But out of curiosity, because I am woman and we are nosey, I wanted to know. He told me he got caught up with the girl in high school, and they lived together because she had a baby. He let me know she didn't have any family, so I knew I couldn't tear them apart at that moment, but I wasn't about to let them be together either. Anyhow, I was also still with my son's father, so I just stayed visible until we were both ready.

I don't know what happened with them, and I never tried to figure it out. But what I did know is not too long afterward, we both ended up single, and he got an apartment in the smaller projects right below where he grew up. One day I called him and told him my son and I were coming over. I didn't ask; I made a statement. As I said, I was always aggressive, and I think that was what attracted him to me. I knew what I wanted, and I always went after it. I was confident, and he knew that about me. On this particular night, I had decided to stay at his house even though I had my own place. You know how "us" ladies do. I wanted to be in his space and see if a girl would come over. Then, I would know my position and play my part.

He loved Chinese food and ordered us his favorite dish: chicken, shrimp, and beef with broccoli.

After we ate, we decided to lie down and chill[6] while he watched the Animal Channel. We all were having a good time enjoying each other's company until later that night.

As I laid beside him, I noticed that his arm was branded. I was furious. I began to bless him out because he was better than that, and he knew it. I called him everything but a child of God. You see, he knew damn well where I was coming from. I asked him why? He did not need to be a part of a gang at all. He came from a big family, so he didn't need a street family. But this made me realize that a big family didn't mean quality relationships. Yet, in my mind, family was family, and that's all that should matter.

The whole situation turned me off, so I left. For the life of me, I couldn't understand why I was upset. It was his choice, and he had to learn on his own. It did not matter what I saw in him; he had to see it for himself. I knew this man had a big heart and a bright future ahead of him. Let me remind you when I say he was a good man; he was just that. But what could I do or say to him? He was just like me— strong-minded. Once he set his mind to something, no one could change it.

As time went on, I needed to move to a different area of the hood that I didn't know, but I didn't have any help. You see in the hood, it's every man for himself. As much as I didn't want to ask my beloved for help, I had too. He was the only one I could count on and I trusted him. I knew he would never allow anything to happen to me or my son. As usual, he was right

[6] Relax or hangout

there, had my back and helped me move into my new apartment. After the move was over, I needed a little free time and wanted to hang out. He babysat my son so that I could. All the little gestures like that made me love him even more. After that move, I didn't hear from him for some time, but that was a pattern for us. Although I was a piece of work, he always wore his heart on his sleeve when it came to me. He understood me and made me feel valid no matter who he was with, what happened, or where he was in life. I respected him for that and knew in my heart that I would owe him my loyalty and love forever. I also knew deep in my heart that he had a life to live, and I had to let him be great. Just as he wasn't ready to leave the streets alone, and I wasn't equipped to deal with him living that lifestyle or subject my son to it.

We reconnected a year or two later and I was not the same young girl he was used to. He was happy to see my growth. Motherhood had changed me. My son was raising me even when I wasn't ready to grow up. So, my mindset was different. I was more mature and evolving as a young woman by the day. He began to visit more frequently, and it was all good for me. I thought I could handle him at this point. I thought I could show him something different in life that would change his mind about the streets.

I loved seeing him and this time it felt right. I couldn't lie to myself. Even though I was involved at the time, I didn't know where that relationship was going. So, I left my options open with him. One day while he was

25

visiting, we were lying in the bed chill'n[7], and the doorbell rang. "Why are your friends at my door?" I asked him. Here we go again, I thought. Why did I think he was going to abandon the street life? Why did I leave myself open for his nonsense?

Ladies and Gentlemen of the jury, I knew at an early age that I was chosen. I wanted to ignore it because sometimes you just want to live on the edge. I knew that I had a special gift from God and the ability to foresee things. I always felt different and still do. To be honest, I was scared of the gift and didn't understand it. Please don't ask me why because I don't have an answer. I just knew in my spirit that him leaving my house that day wasn't the right thing to do. I told him that I did not have a good feeling about him going, but of course, he was a grown man and had to do what he had to do. He was more than loyal, and that was a quality that attracted me to him. The question was, at what cost? Nevertheless, he went on his way, and *YES* he got in trouble on that same day. I know you're wondering what happened, but that's not my story to tell, so stay on track. This story is for me to help other women like me, so keep listening.

"REMEMBER TO HOLD ONTO YOURSELF WHILE HOLDING

ONTO HIM"

---

[7] Hanging out, relax mode or do nothing

COUSIN

As time passed, I started hearing my beloved was gangbanging[8], but I didn't say anything. I just kept minding his business without his knowledge. I was still tight with his cousin, so I knew everything that was going on with him. She was like one of my best friends, a sister, really. I loved her to death. My best friend and I were both too grown before our time. Her brother would always say, "y'all just alike with those bad attitudes" Yeah! We just didn't play around, but the difference with me was I was a go-getter. Even though I saw that in her, I guess she didn't see it in herself at the time. On the other hand, sometimes people can see what you have and become jealous. We ended up having a falling out just because someone took a conversation back to my friend out of context. You guessed it. Our friendship went downhill from there. I learned that sometimes family will hurt you faster than the next man on the street. I also learned that when you're going through any life-changing event: stress, depression, financial hardship, or lack of support, it can leave great people stagnant and prevent them from operating at their fullest potential. I recognized my best friend's greatness when we were just kids. I was just expressing to the hater how I couldn't understand why she (my friend/sister) didn't see it? I should have been more cautious venting. Everybody is not genuine, nor

---

[8] Violent act(s) committed by a gang or gangbanger

do they belong in your personal space. But this person was an old friend of ours. We had just reunited with her, and I didn't think she could be so evil. I guess speaking about it with the wrong person came across as I was coming from a negative place, but that was so far from the truth. But you live and learn. It was never my intention to bring any harm to my best friend. Just like I knew she wouldn't bring any harm to me. She was always there for me like when I needed help packing to move into one of the new houses built under the city's revitalization project. I didn't know how I was going to pay the astronomical rent, but I knew I could count on her. It was her day off and I went to pick her up. We sat in the old house, folded clothes, and packed up boxes. We laughed, we joked, and we played. In the end, we had a good time. I would have never thought that days later, I would lose my childhood friend over a misunderstanding. My best friend didn't even allow me to express this to her. I thought we were better than that.

Ladies and Gentlemen of the jury, when you're going through things, you can't hear the truth, nor do you want to listen to it. We all have been there, and if you haven't already, you will. This hurt me badly; it was like I lost a piece of myself when I lost her. Yet, time goes on, and I learned to live with the fact that sometimes you outgrow people and people outgrow you. Sometimes situations cause division, and friendships get displaced. One thing about me, when I love, I love hard. You know that love I'm speaking of, that unconditional love. I am a cheerleader for my friends and want my team to be great and win in life. The thought of my friend going through hard times bothered me. Ladies and Gentlemen of the jury, the moral of the story is that we must stay in tune with ourselves even when we are going through difficulties. Despite it all, she proved she still loved me because my babe, (that didn't listen to me), asked her to contact me while she was still mad. She was gracious enough to put her anger aside to unite our love. I will forever be grateful for her selfless act to support us. She told me that my Boo was serving ten years in the state prison for the incident on the day he left my house. Ten years, OMG! I couldn't believe my ears. She asked if it was ok for her to give him my number. Quiet as kept, I missed him, so I let her know it was ok. At that point, he already served about three and a half years. I thought I didn't want to be bothered, but I wanted to prove to him he should have listened to me. Now, Ladies and Gentlemen of the jury, you know that's how we do. "Yeah... I told you so," but my heart couldn't deny how I truly felt. I know that when women fall in love, we can become blind at the same time. I still loved him regardless of whether he was in my life, out of my life, or with or without someone. I knew I would always love him. We were inseparable. To this day, I don't even think his cousin knew how much I loved her because of this. The truth of the matter is, if it weren't for her putting her feelings aside and calling me, I would have probably never reconnected with my "now" husband. Thank you, cousin!

VISIT TIME

By this time, we were talking every day. He owned a cell phone behind the prison walls. Of course, it could have generated a new charge if he were caught, but he wanted to talk, and we did. He was happy to hear my voice and vice versa. Once the soap opera General Hospital went off, I knew his call was sure to follow. While it may seem funny, he said that watching the stories helped him keep up with the time and whatever year in his bid[9] he was doing. Interesting right? I was still trying to be strong, but I had a weak moment listening to his reasoning. Yes, I was falling weak in love. Somehow it happened without my rational thoughts or understanding.

Finally, he asked me to visit. I said yes without hesitation. In the back of my mind during all the calls, I was already planning to wear my cutest outfit and do my hair. You know, look all the way good. I told myself I would look like somebody out of a magazine, and he wasn't going ever want to let me go. Well, during our first visit, I did look good, but the rest of the plan backfired on me. I didn't want to let him go either— game over at this point. "WE" were both all in. Let me repeat that again, Ladies and Gentlemen of the jury, "WE" were all in. However, I wish he would have listened to me so he wouldn't have been behind bars. How many of y'all understand that the sentence was a part of GOD's plan?

---

[9] Slang term for prison sentence

No matter what, he was always faithful and true to me. He proved to me that love is unconditional. We were then at the four-year mark, with six more to go. Girl...a ten-year stretch. Damn... it seemed like that was so far off. I began to do time with him, and it went so fast I didn't even realize I was doing it.

"REMEMBER TO HOLD ONTO YOURSELF WHILE HOLDING ONTO HIM"

Now! I must tell you, although I wasn't behind bars, I was locked-up too. Visitation became second nature to me. It was my new normal. I had no clue that I was becoming institutionalized just like him. I started getting up early to get ready for my three to four-hour ride, depending on the traffic flow. I had to find my son a babysitter and everything else that goes along with it, like: making sure I had coins to get snacks from the vending machine because outside food wasn't permitted or extra clothes in the trunk of my car just in case the correctional officer (CO) wanted to deny my visit because he didn't like my outfit; or the underwire needed to be cut out of my bra to avoid the security scanner from going off. I have huge boobies, so this was a lot to sacrifice because my bras are far from cheap. I started doing all these things naturally, but I never lost my mind. At visit time, our conversations would be about our future. He understood that he had to accept the responsibilities of becoming the head of the house:

HIM: I can't wait to get home and take care of y'all.

ME: How are you going to take care of me? We need to have an action plan in place because I am designed to be a helpmate.

HIM: Oh, you think I'm not strong enough to take care of my family.

ME: Do you think the world stopped for you? Do you think that is just going to be that easy to pick life back up right where you left it?

I would have to bring him back to reality and say that he would have lost a decade of his life once he returned home that he could not get back. He was pissed off when I asked if he thought it was going to be that easy. Think about it... life was standing still for him but was constantly moving outside the prison walls. It was most definitely going to be a task, and I knew that. We talked about what he wanted to do for a living and discussed stocks and bonds. I was attracted to that. We were learning to build a life together and not with fast money.[10] Another major topic we discussed was about having more kids. In my mind, that was a no go. It may come across as selfish to some, but for me, it was my truth. Keep in mind, his son was two when he went to prison and a pre-teen when he came home. He missed out on his whole childhood. The new baby wasn't to

---

[10] Money earned by selling drugs

forget or replace the child he had, but to experience what he never did. Although these topics were frustrating, we had to habitually discuss them to make our life after prison successful. We both needed to know that there was a light at the end of this tunnel, and I needed to feel safe and secure.

"REMEMBER TO HOLD ONTO YOURSELF WHILE HOLDING ONTO HIM"

NOTE: *I don't have to go into details. You get what I am trying to say, so stop judging him. Because if you keep living, you will experience that sometimes life just isn't fair but REAL! Keep living.*

MY SON FROM ANOTHER MOTHER

One day, Babe called me to tell me his son's birthday was coming up and he wanted me to buy a gift on his behalf. His son was only two years old when he went to prison. At this point, his son was growing up fast, and he was missing out. Now, I am the girlfriend with the child blending a family before I recognized I was blending a family. It came so naturally. I was just moving along and asking God to order my footsteps while praying not to lose myself in the process. He asked me to get his son a Nextel phone. At that time, all the kids were getting them, and he wanted his son to have one too. I had money like that back then, so it was nothing for me to buy one.

On the day of his birthday, I wrapped the gift and brought a balloon and card to his son's school that said LOVE DAD. I got a ride by one of my friends, so I did not have to look for parking. When I arrived, I didn't know how to feel or what to expect. But I stayed focused on the task and delivered the gift per my Babe's request. I introduced myself as Tah, his dad's girlfriend, and told him that his father wanted me to get him something for his birthday. When he opened the gift and saw the Nextel phone, his face lit up. Seeing the look on his face was priceless. I was taken aback and fell in love with that kid right then. I didn't realize what I was doing; it happened so fast. I didn't even process if what I was doing was right or wrong. Thinking back, I know how I would have felt if I were his son's mother. I would have been angry if someone went to see my child. To top it off, someone I knew. Personally, I would have gone inside my son's school and flipped out. Even though his father connected me to the godmother, the mother should have been allowed to approve my visit first. The funny part is, I told the front office his dad was locked-up, and I wanted to do something special for him; they were down for the cause too. But shouldn't they have called the mother to verify? I am just saying. Yet all went well, and I left my number and told him to have his mother contact me to discuss spending time with my son and me in the future. This was the beginning of our relationship. There was no turning back.

I began to take his son and mine on my prison visits. We were all growing together. I was preparing for his exit, so I thought. It used to make me so happy to have all of us together when we visited. The boys had a strong bond like they knew each other forever. It was amazing. On the visits, his son would be so loud and say... "Tah is a rich girl. Dad, did you know that?" I didn't want the wrong ear to hear it,) to get robbed or hit upside my head. I knew he didn't mean any harm, but we never know what people are capable of. His dad would talk to him, after all, we were still in a prison, and everybody was suspect.

It was just so amazing to see our family blending with genuine ease as we were preparing for marriage. I know you're thinking I should be preparing for the wedding, but I said it right. The wedding ceremony is only one day of a marriage that is supposed to last a lifetime. So YES! I was preparing for the marriage. I had to make sure that we were going to be good because I went from not wanting to be bothered to him becoming my world. So, remember to hold onto yourself while you're holding on to him.

At this point, I am doing time with him but still living my best life: traveling, shopping, and making money. I never shortchanged myself. Pay attention and hear me clearly. I never stopped taking care of myself. I had to tell myself that. I still had to live my life regardless of the circumstances. But when I tell you my husband is the last of the Dying Breed, he is just that. He would say to me, I know you're going to go out and do what you want to do, but there are two rules to the game: don't bring back any diseases and don't fall in love. I respected the game and lived my life just like that. I didn't feel like somebody was holding me back, but instead, he gave me something to look forward to. I started feeling like a dude, getting what I could get out of them and being on my merry way. Yup! I was hustling money from guys left and right. Don't act like I am the only one. I can see your body language that you're judging me. So stop it. I told you in the beginning, I had a certain lifestyle to maintain quietly. On top of making my own money, the drug world was fast cash with easy access.

Each visit made it harder for me to live that life, and I was convicted spiritually and emotionally. It was no longer a high for me to hustle guys out of their money. I had my own money and a mindset to create extra income if I needed it. I always thought like a boss, but the shorter his time got, the less desire I had to play games. Who knew that GOD was preparing me for my Boaz? It definitely gave me something to think about. I was able to think about the good man that made a wrong decision. I was able to kind of process what was going on.

I was a sucker for the kids, and they knew it. Whatever they wanted, I would make it my business to try and make it happen. However, the boys knew I would discipline them too. I only knew how to have fun, so my punishment was not being able to eat out. One weekend when his son came over, and I took the kids out to eat. He asked why we were going out because he was used to going out only when he did something special. That meant so much to me. He was able to identify being rewarded for something. He was helping me and didn't even understand it. I loved that kid so much. Me and the boys would do all types of fun stuff together. He added so much to me and my son's life, especially my son. As an only child, he was the brother my son never had. My son was into skateboarding, so he would teach his "step-brother" how to ride, and my "stepson" was into basketball, so would he show my son a little bit of that. Everything was working out. The only thing that was missing was my love, who was still behind bars.

THE DEVIL THOUGHT HE HAD ME

I knew one day we would reach a point where we would start a life together outside the prison walls. We always talked about our life after prison, and he would say to me at every visit, you know I don't want to live in New Jersey, right? I knew he wanted to relocate so he could have a fresh start. Was I really ready? He gave me comfort by considering my need to be near family. So, we jointly decided that when he came home, we would move to North Carolina where my mother lived. He was already used to living without family, so this decision was a no brainer for him.

When we talked about relocating during visits, it all sounded good to me. I never stopped to think about how my life would be impacted if I decided to move. I just went along with the plan while he was in prison, and I knew that somehow someway it would all work out *(my way, of course)*. But after the visit, I would go home, back to my reality, and replay our conversations in my head. I would say in my mind, "girl, you can't leave; this is where your money is; how are you going to pick up and leave?" I was so confused. The devil started playing with my mind, or was it God, testing my faith? Although, I was ready for a change, I wasn't willing to surrender my lifestyle. You see, sometimes we get so consumed with ourselves, we never stop to think about anyone else *(I had to learn this as time went on)*. Sometimes when you're sitting in a situation, you can't see what's really going on around you. Stop judging me before I finish telling my story. I promise you that you will see how God started to handle me without warning a little bit at a time.

Life was good. My son's father was "finding himself," so I only had me to depend on. I had to make life happen for my son. My mother would visit me from time to time. Keep in mind I was living in a brand-new house. I was the first person to ever sit on the toilet. I was paying market rent, and I felt good about the life I created for my only child and me. I converted a room into a hair studio to make it comfortable for my clients and I was making money in the comfort of my home. I never had Section-8 to rely on or any form of government assistance. Not that there's anything wrong with it, but God knows it wasn't for me. It would have likely hindered me rather than helped me. I was following my mother's footsteps my way.

However, no matter how new the house was, I was still in the hood. I had blinders on and couldn't see anything but my money and a new home. But when my mother would come, she made sure she subtly reminded me that I was still in the hood. Now, she wouldn't dare come out and say it because I had a mouth on me, but her facial expressions would say it all without her uttering one word. She would turn her nose up into the air, and I would say things to her like, "you need to stop; you act like you have never lived here before" or "Oh! You think you're better than the hood since you moved out?"

I guess this is what my husband was thinking too. I was not hearing or paying attention to the fact that life was better for her, and I was stuck. The money had me enslaved without knowing. I didn't understand then that it was more to life than just money, riding in a new Mercedes Benz, and living in a new house in the hood. I was wasting money unintentionally; I was setting myself up for failure. I was so consumed with living a glamorous life; I never considered I was living in a rat race with no return on my investment. I didn't have the time to sit still to even hear God's voice. But look at how God commanded his authority in my life. He positioned me to be still without me understanding His approach. He sent a man in prison as a decoy to get my attention. I didn't realize it then, but God is so powerful. I mean, He is so creative. Wow! Look at God. Pay close attention to the story. It is not ALL about the man in prison, you see, but the transformation of my mind that was in prison too. Keep reading until it makes sense.

"REMEMBER TO HOLD ONTO YOURSELF WHILE HOLDING ONTO HIM"

God was using me as a tool to help my husband, but he was also using my husband as a tool to free me. Sometimes when you're making money, life with God becomes per diem or as needed. Hear me clearly. I always praised and worshipped God, but it wasn't consistent. I can be honest with myself. I was hustling hard when God already had my back. All I had to do was call on Him and ask. The devil was having a good time with me. I wasn't paying my tithes. I was just living what I thought was my best life, NOT. No dollar was ever enough. I was too busy worrying about how I was going to maintain my lifestyle with bills that were almost 5K per month. I made money, but enough was never enough. I should have been saving, but guess what, nobody ever told me about credit. I had to learn it on my own; nobody ever told me about savings, and I had to learn that on my own too. I made money like a drug dealer. That's why I was attracted to those types of men. The money came easy, so I spent it fast with no regrets. My only thoughts were, "I'll get it back tomorrow," without even understanding what tomorrow held.

I knew how to pray, and I went to church every Sunday, but it was only behavioral because I knew I *had* to go to church. Yet, I was missing the part where I needed to practice what I learned in church. I was living a worldly life, not applying the Word of God. Instead, I gravitated to the things in the world (cars, money, clothes, all along knowing God was able to supply what I needed and wanted. Stop judging me. I was going through my own spiritual warfare. I had to re-learn how to meditate on God's Word. The difference is when you're living a godly life, things in the world change, but the Word of God always stays the same. I was praying, but I didn't understand how to pray and sit and wait for God to answer. I loved the Lord, but I had to put in the work if I wanted a return from God. I needed to learn how to pray to the Lord because it's what is required and wait on Him to respond. I needed to find a mental space to meditate and remove myself from the ways of the world. I just didn't understand how. I needed to fully recognize that I needed the Lord.

THE TRANSFER

My husband received a date to be transferred to a state prison facility 15 minutes from my house. We were so happy. I was happy because I hated taking those long rides and burning up my gas. My soon to be mother-in-law was going to miss those rides because she lived closer to the other facility. I would pick her up, and we would just cruise along. Quiet as kept, I was going to miss them too because it was our private time together. Aside from his son, she was the only family member that would go with me and visit. When we left the visits, we would stop at Roy Roger's fast-food restaurant. That was our spot. Those were the good old days. But that was all over. I was so excited. This was a turning point for us. This meant that our time was short, and he would be coming home soon. YESSSS!! It felt good that I didn't have to compromise rescheduling my clients or miss out on my money to go on visits hours away. It felt good being 15 minutes away. God is so good. His blessings continued. Then, when the time was allowed, he was able to apply for a transfer to the re-entry house.

RE-ENTRY PROGRAM

It was on now! He was approved to go into the re-entry house, a cross between a prison with barbed wire and a halfway house. There, they could dress like a civilian. They also had a little more freedom and learned communication skills. This was a step in the right direction; he was becoming re-acclimated into society one day at a time. Although I was excited about him coming closer to home, (one foot out of the prison and one foot in the world), the reality was I felt scared, nervous, anxious, overwhelmed, and confused. This was now becoming a reality. All the time I had been visiting, I never worried about anyone bombarding my visits because out of sight out of mind. However, once everyone found out, the "CARING" calls began to come through. His aunt on his father's side called me when it was time for him to be transferred to the re-entry house. She asked me if she could go with me to drop-off my husband's care package. I replied, "sure no problem," but in the back of my mind why now? I have to be honest with myself, my thoughts, and my feelings! Nonetheless, she came and never once did she or anyone else for that matter offer to help me get his care package in order. No worries though because I always handled my business, besides, he was about to be my husband, so I had his back no matter what. I was on a mission, we had goals, and reaching our goals was a priority. Pause from the story a second. I want you Ladies and Gentlemen of the jury to really understand that it takes two people to plan goals for them to work. If you're not working as one unit, the relationship after prison (any relationship) will fail. I don't care how much you have visited, how much commissary you dropped on his books, or how faithful you were. If he is not committed to doing the work, you will be fighting a losing battle. I want you to remember this point if nothing else.

OK back to the story. I knew early in the game that if I had to walk away from this, I could and still be whole. Once I knew he was committed to executing the plan that we had established, I was really all in, hands down; there was no turning back. But was I really ready? I had to be. His time was getting shorter and we were faced with the reality of him coming home. I needed to know that the argument we had early on, *"You think I can't take care of my family"* would come to pass. I wanted him to live up to his promise, *"I can't wait to take care of y'all..."*

I will never forget this part of his transition. The time was approaching fast. Could he really handle it? There were so many feelings running through my mind. I would remind him that he only had a couple of months to stay in the reentry transitional house before going to the halfway house. I don't know how the halfway house works where you are from, but in New Jersey, you're required to have a job in order to be at the halfway house or at least that is the goal. They give you time to find a job and the agency has joint partnerships with different companies.

FAMILY INCENTIVE PROGRAM

They had a highly effective program for women like me, supporters, prison wives, and girlfriends. A family incentive program took place every Monday at around 6 pm, right after everyone got off work. We met with other women waiting for their significant other to come home in a small conference room. They would show videos that gave examples of real-life situations that women may encounter when their partner came home. These videos showed how men would come home depressed and feel down on themselves. These videos about family relationships and marriage hit home for me. I can't speak for anyone else, but I was processing this information because he was now in the residential re-entry program. I was ignorant to assume that other women in the room wanted to learn. But they just wanted that extra visit.

One thing that I knew for sure was that I would never get married behind bars. I was worth more. I would never start off in marriage, feeling like I was robbed of my childhood dream. The reality was that he was incarcerated with no exit date. I thank God for allowing me to be true to myself. For me, I needed those memories. I knew he wanted to have more children and I couldn't process sharing our wedding pictures behind bars. All I could think about was if I had a daughter, what expectations would I be setting for her. I envisioned being able to pass my dress down to her and teach her how to love unconditionally. However, I also would be teaching her never to lower her standards. You see, it's easy to come down to someone's level, but it takes hard work to bring people up to yours.

Moving forward, after our meetings, we were able to have dinner and discuss our wedding plans. I would always make him feel inclusive with the plans. This gave him something to look forward to. We would talk about the colors. He was in love with all colors I chose. My favorite colors were Tiffany blue and chocolate. Once we agreed on colors, I would get little things for samples, and we would have fun planning our wedding together.

I helped him regain hope and understanding that there was life after prison. We were heading in the right direction, and this process was working. Twelve months after being in the residential re-entry house, he got his second approval. We were now going to the halfway house! The halfway house was nice. It was located on a residential street and blended in with the community. It had a beautiful front and backyard for the guys to enjoy. The guys would even cookout sometimes. It had a feeling of being home, but it wasn't our home yet. What an amazing feeling to know that he made it through nine years (six for me) and only one year left to complete in the halfway house. It all seemed surreal. At this point in my life, the love was growing more profound. I can be real with myself. I had my guard up, and I was nervous about him coming home and switching up on me. At this point, I had to protect my heart and open my eyes and my ears. I needed God to confirm if this man was indeed my

Boaz. I had to use my discerning spirit to guide me through because my emotions would have controlled my mind, and I couldn't allow that to happen.

Psalm 119:125 New International Version (NIV)
I am your servant; give me discernment
that I may understand your statutes.

MY CLIENTS WERE MY FAMILY

I cannot express to you enough how my clients were people that genuinely cared about me and my son's welfare. I had a strong networking circle that included some highly respected people. These were the people that I fellowshipped with every day of my life. You see, I never wanted that "Fly Girl" base clientele. My target audience was a more mature and professional class of women. I wanted to level up, and I believe you become the company you keep. These women were my mentors; they were grooming me and didn't even know it. They helped me understand politics, education, and that networking was a powerful tool in life and business.

This prominent group of women didn't know why I wanted to date a man in prison. However, it didn't matter; they supported me and became my human resource center. I will forever love each one of them. Doing prison time was already hard, but to have their support meant everything to me. I know you're probably saying, "why did she even care," but to know these women was to love them. My clients were my family, they were my lifeline. They always had my back; they were loyal and showed unconditional love to my son and me. These women knew that I was strong and trusted God. This was one of those situations that I had to put my trust in Him. But they were my human tools of support that I needed.

TRUSTING GOD

I understand that God should order everything we do. We might not understand it while we're doing it or when we're doing it. And we don't have to. All we have to do is be obedient to the word of God, and I was doing just that. I love God. But for so long, I wasn't applying the Word of God the way that I should have been. I thank God for looking out for the babies and fools. I was a baby spiritually, a fool to the world. So, guess what? God looked out for me. He was planting seeds! I didn't understand what was going on in my life, but I trusted the process. I was super excited about what was next. I can't lie. On the inside, I was filled with fear of the unknown. Ladies and Gentlemen of the jury, you have to be honest with yourself. It's ok to have these feelings; it is proof that you're in touch with your inner self; stay WOKE![11]

Jeremiah 29:11 New International Version (NIV)
11 For I know the plans I have for you," declares the Lord, "plans to prosper you and not to harm you plans to give you hope and a future.

---

[11] To be aware/conscience of what is going on around you at all times

MY NETWORK IS MY NET WORTH

After receiving the confirmation from God that I was on the right path, I began to wear my heart on my sleeve. I was all in. I began to set him up for SUCCESS after prison. He had to become the head of our lives. He was the hunter, and I needed him to lead just like I knew he could. I knew his worth, but the question was, did he? So, I pulled out my Rolodex and started making calls to get a job set in place for him. To share my network, I had to really trust a person. Keep in mind, I already had wood burning in the fire for him based on the action plan we had created. However, until I had removed all doubts, I was coasting.

One of my clients, unlike the others, was more around my age range. She became more like my a sister. She and I would discuss his release and about him getting a job. She would always say, "Tisha (that was what she called me), he's going to be alright; we got you, which means we got him." So, because of the love they had for me, it overflowed and poured into the love they had for my Babe. I now had the confidence to seal the deal; we positioned him to walk right into a job. Not just any job, but a job with benefits: medical, vision, and dental. They even had an incentive pay for showing up for work on time every thirty days. My network was truly setting him up for SUCCESS. They were nervous for me. They knew I was hard-headed. They knew it didn't matter what they said to me. I took what I needed from their opinion and threw the rest back. Most of my clients were older and looked at me like a daughter. I got it. That is why I always heard their voice and listened respectfully. I always had a strong mind, and for the most part, I made the right decisions. Especially when God gave me the green light to move. I felt like the rapper Remy Ma... "Nothing can stop me; I am all the way up." Once he made it to the halfway house, he had to go through the clearance process before he could start his job search. No worries because his job was secured and ready to go.

SPACE & OPPORTUNITY

Well, well, well, the day came, and he got his opportunity to hit the streets. It was heaven. We didn't immediately go job hunting because we had that part in place. You guessed it; we were stealing time[12]... stop judging us... we're human. All that came to my mind was, "Lord forgive us because we are about to sin." This may not be right, but I'm just being transparent and telling you our truth. We were living in every moment together and never thought of the consequences. Once, we released those warm feelings of affection pinned up inside of us, we were back to business. We started working on his license, photo ID, birth certificate, social security card, taxes, etc. Yes! It was much work, but we had to get it done, and we did.

It wasn't an easy process; in fact, we had a hard time with the IRS. They were harassing him about unfiled taxes for years he was incarcerated. I had to keep him calm; the anxiety was setting in. I told him, "Don't worry, I will get it worked out," and I did. It was second nature to make life happen for him. I didn't realize that I was spoiling him. They say how you start is the way to finish. This is definitely true. On the other hand, he spoiled me too. That is why I never lowered my standard for him. Instead, he rose to mine. While he was in prison, he was stacking his money, knowing we planned to get married. He wanted the luxury of being able to

---

[12] Maximizing the time allotted to handle business or work by avoiding taking public transportation to ride in a personal vehicle without authorization.

purchase me a ring on his own. That meant everything to me. He was starting our life together on the right foot. One day he said:

HIM: Take me to the bank to make a withdrawal."

ME: BANK?

HIM: Yes, I set up an account while I was in prison.

I didn't hesitate. I rushed him to the bank like he asked. Once we grabbed the cash, he asked me to take him to where I had seen the ring I wanted. I liked that kind of talk. Talk that talk, Babe. When we went into the jewelry store, I showed him the ring, and without hesitation, he purchased it. I was so excited to finally get my ring on my finger that my crazy self didn't realize he was on his knee asking me to marry him. I was acting a damn fool. I was in such disbelief because all we ever talked about was coming to fruition. Of course, I said yes. This may not be romantic to you, but it was for me. Let me help you to see the romance. He just came home after a decade in prison and spent his entire savings to assure me that his words were genuine. That meant the world to me because you never know which way a man will go after you did his time as a prison wife. Babe likes to call it, "a prison hangover." Thank God his word was his bond. He's a real "G[13]

---

[13] Gangsta/Partner/Friend,

THERE'S WORK TO BE DONE

My Babe was now ready to claim that job that was waiting on him. He was making $15.00 an hour. Let's just talk about that for a minute. We are talking about 2007. Some people don't even make $15.00 an hour now. He was definitely in a good position. Here is where it became tricky. Ladies and Gentlemen of the jury, these men have been locked up for so long that they don't want anyone telling them what to do. However, in life, we always have to follow somebody's rules. He also hated the job's hard labor, but it was a job and the open door to his freedom. I was now beginning to observe his behaviors.

Thank you, Lord, for keeping me aware. That "Honeymoon Release" was fading away fast. I had to think quickly. I trusted God, and He gave me wisdom, and it was now time to use it. I had to become the structure for Babe because I foresaw how easy it could be for him to stray. I had to stay on him to keep him on task because he hated this job. Hate it or not, it opened up opportunities for him once he completed his time at the halfway house. Yet, he had no value for this job. It wasn't that he didn't want to work. It just wasn't the type of job he wanted to do. With that said, he found everything he could that was wrong with the job. Ladies and Gentlemen of the jury pay attention. This is one of the many things we don't think about while our man is serving time. If I wasn't on his back, he could have easily given up and maybe even start to feel unworthy. But this was not an option. I could now see why God was grooming me to be his strength while he was finding himself.

Yet trying to be his supporter without becoming his correctional office became hard. The truth was that if he fell short, I was his correctional officer. I saw his greatness and was not going to stand by and allow him to make bad choices that he would regret later. I know some may be thinking this and saying he's grown that's on him. The reality is after being locked-up for so long, too much freedom would have been overwhelming for him. You don't have to believe me, but surveys don't lie. However, I became his human conscience and his calm all at the same time.

THE PRISON AFTERMATH BEGINS

Once men return from prison, they have first to understand and accept the reality of what they now have to live through. Even so, this is the beginning of their rehabilitation. You may think I'm crazy but, this is true. He is not okay. Yet, he will come home with the illusion of who he is and what he wants to do, but he can't fool himself for long. The facade will fall, and his true inner self is going to show up. Imagine someone micromanaging someone every second of the day. Then, you get a little bit of freedom while trying to learn how to balance having one foot back in society and the other foot still under state custody.

Picture this for a second, not being able to express yourself for a decade. I mean, really, how would you feel? All of these feelings are boxed up with nowhere to escape, and you have to learn how to have feelings again. Let me go a little deeper. He was used to being told what to do while locked up, so being told what to do outside of prison was a hard adjustment. I assume, it was a reminder of what he had been through while incarcerated. So, this was something we had to work on.

Failure to follow the rules comes with a consequence. We all have to listen to somebody. For example, if we have a driver's license, we have to obey the traffic rules. If we run a red light, we will get a ticket. I had to help him understand that life is different for him now, and the jobs he was used to were going to be hard to come by. I also helped him see that he is in charge of his destiny and had to stick with a job until something else came through. I was helping him to learn how to think logically again. This was not an easy process, but I was so proud of him because he wanted to learn how to control impulses. He was learning how to think before he reacted, and he was growing. That was a must. I'm not saying all men will deal with this, but it will depend on the time spent in prison and his mental capacity. Most men that go to prison are usually smart, creative, and very intellectual. However, having these talents have been compromised for long periods of time and can be overwhelming for you and him. Being re-acclimated back into society is hard work for the formerly incarcerated and his partner.

They have to learn how to pay bills and find that balance in life. This is the purpose of the halfway house. Some that return home from prison may have a stack of old money (don't act like you don't understand what I mean), drug money. Some may argue that this is not true. However, the truth is that money keeps them from dealing with reality. I can't speak for all men, but for the most part, camouflaging their behaviors is an effect of mass incarceration. Money doesn't heal them; it only prolongs and suppresses their real recovery. This applies to men in or out of prison.

REALITY CHECK

Yeah, I made good money, but maintaining my lifestyle wasn't an easy task. All my money was accounted for. I paid market rent, high car notes on my luxury cars, and expensive car insurance to match. I paid all my bills, not to mention bought clothes and shoes to keep up my appearance while taking care of my child. I never stopped to think about how this would affect him when he came home. He had unrealistic expectations of what he could do. The only thing on my mind was him saying, "so you think I can't take care of my family?" But the truth was he didn't make enough money to take care of the family. It was going to be a process for him to reach not instant gratification. I had to mentally wrap my head around this because this was programmed in my mind. Prison talk is real!

MENTAL NOTE: *Surveys show that men want to come home and resume full responsibility for the household. However, it's unrealistic, and most men revert into their old lifestyles unless he has drug money stored away, comes from a family of money, or hit the lottery. I'm just being real!*

Honestly, I never thought about how he hadn't worked in 10 years or how rent had increased over a decade. He only lived in subsidized housing before prison, so I never thought how this would intimidate him as a man. All I could think about was the Bible verse that says I am the helpmate.

Genesis 2:18 New International Version (NIV)
18 The Lord God said, "It is not suitable for the man to be alone. I will make a helper suitable for him."

It is funny how we can pull the verses out to accommodate our wants. Did this verse fit the situation in which we were living? Let me be clear, this doesn't mean to lower your expectations, just be considerate of his reality. No matter what, I was not depriving him of his role as head of household, but it was something we had to work towards. Ladies and Gentlemen of the jury, I want you to be aware of how this can make him feel inadequate as a man. At this point, I didn't understand the signs of depression. I never thought about him experiencing Post-Traumatic Stress Disorder (PTSD). I have always attributed these mental issues to men being in the military. I never thought about PTSD being part of life after prison. Now I see they are one in the same. I became self-taught about mental health. I researched, read, analyzed, and learned what he was going through. I didn't understand immediately. I learned this over a period of time. And I didn't realize that I started to lose myself in the interim. I was overwhelmed and didn't know it.

"REMEMBER TO HOLD ONTO YOURSELF WHILE HOLDING ONTO HIM"

WE LOVED OUR HALFWAY HOUSE FAMILY

Babe was spending most of his time on the streets, and we were moving and shaking. We were working as a team and having fun while doing so. I was so caught up making sure that he was straight, that I was falling deeper in love as the days went by. He became my lifestyle. To be honest, he was only really at the halfway house so they could account for the inmates in their custody or make "count," as it is called. I would walk into the halfway house with my bubbly personality and being the person that I am, people were naturally drawn to me. As they say, I never meet a stranger. The receptionist started making small talk with me and wanted to know what I did for a living. After she learned she learned that I was a hairstylist, we exchanged numbers. She later called me to schedule an appointment. I'm all smiles at that moment. The funniest thing was that as an employee of the halfway house she could not legally fraternize with the inmates. Although she was not directly fraternizing with an inmate, she mingled with an inmate's relative and visited the parolee's home address to get her hair done. However, that didn't stop business and did not stunt the growth of our developing relationship. She liked my bubbly and outgoing personality, and we are still friends till this day. There must be a God! Keep reading.

There was a second lady attendant at the halfway house who was the driver. This woman worked with my mother at the hospital back in the day. When she first saw me, she said she remembered me as a kid wearing a Catholic school uniform. She would drive the working inmates to the mall, movies, restaurants, or wherever they would agree upon. She began to tell me where to meet them so that I could pick up my Babe. She was helping us to spend more private time together while they were out on their field trips. This game became easier by the day. I know you're wondering, why did I trust her? I knew she wouldn't report us because our time together was freeing up her time to have relations with one of the other inmates. It was great. She also had to allow the other gentlemen the same privilege we had. All I could think was, "Is this shit real?" There was a third worker that helped us too. He was the father of the client who had helped my Babe get the job. So, we had all the work shifts covered.

You heard me right your Honor. The way I saw it, it was a fair exchange and no robbery. When I think back, we were taking a big gamble. Nowadays, I would be so scared to do these types of things. Can you see how God has worked in me? That is nothing but the conviction of God that lives in me today.

LET THE CREDIT BEGIN

Now that you know whose who, you can see how each attendant played a role in our lives. Thank God we had their help or was it the devil? The pressure was on. Now it was time for the hard work to begin. He had to live up to all that he told me he would do. He just needed support to navigate his path. I held him accountable because I knew he could be the man I needed him to be. One thing for sure, I wasn't going to allow anyone to sabotage all of our hard work or my sacrifices. My mind was totally on making sure that he stayed focused. After all, the key to our success was staying committed to the plan we created together. He always made it to count to look good on paper. This was definitely fun. We were taking a chance, but it gave us so much excitement, and it showed us that we could be team players. . We loved the fact that he was able to spend more time at with me and just 'woosah' for a minute or two. We had a bond that couldn't be broken. I could curse him out, and he would curse me out, but no one else better dare try it. We were two peas in a pod.

We got his license reinstated, and we felt ready to tackle whatever was next. But before we did, he asked if he could drive my car. I was anal about my car. However, I let him drive. This was one of the happiest days of his life. He began to cry, thanking me for believing in him and allowing him to drive my car. It was an eye-opener for me because things that were a huge deal for him were insignificant to me. With this in mind, I wanted those tears of joy to last a lifetime. We started to discuss establishing credit and getting him a car of his very own. One thing about me, I wasn't crazy enough to put anything in my name for anyone. I learned enough about credit that I had to protect myself until I was confident enough to know that he respected credit too. One day before going to work, I made arrangements to take him to a car dealership.

The plans were set in place to avoid any write-ups that could send him back to the state penitentiary. We had to be on point. We found a Jeep Cherokee, and he fell in love with that truck. We presented his paystubs, photo ID, and signed the deal, and he made it to work on time. Keep in mind he had a car payment now; he is mathematically inclined. He understood the magic of money and how to make it work with his income records at the halfway house. You thought we were stealing time before; we were really stealing time now. I didn't have to get up and run him around; he now had full access to do this independently. Maaaaaan, that felt good!

HALFWAY HOUSE FIRST ATTENDANT

Remember the halfway house receptionist that wanted her hair done? Well, she was now a regular client, but he didn't know yet and neither did she. I needed the connection with all of us to be organic. He was shocked when he walked into my work area to greet me and saw her. He looked like he wanted to shit on himself. I guess she was a bit blown away too. I could have shared this information with both of them. However, would either one of them have come? Probably not, I needed to establish trust first in order for it to work and it did.

In all fairness, they were both in violation. What I knew to be true was that she didn't want to lose her job, so she wasn't going to report him. He didn't want to go back to state prison, so he wasn't going to tell on her either. Not to mention, snitching is not in our DNA. Anyway, the receptionist was able to relate to the rules of the game a little more clearly. Although they were both in a state of shock, they were relieved all at the same time. I wish you could have been a fly on the wall. With that being said, we all moved forward and broke bread. Maaaan! We loved her. She is still the coolest of them all.

NO MORE SNEAK'N & CREEP'N

Finally, the day came. We loaded the car and pulled off, so fast we left skid marks in the street. YESSSSS... he had been released. It smells like freedom to me! I felt like Martin Luther King for a minute, "FREE AT LAST, FREE AT LAST, THANK GOD ALMIGHTY, HE IS FREE AT LAST." When we walked into the house for the first time (without looking over our shoulder), I was filled with all types of emotions.

I was elated that he was home, yet anxious all at the same time because he was not 100% free. After a few days of waking up in the same bed together looking at each other eye to eye, we knew that we still had to meet the parole officer, DAMN! Once they have you in the system, the waiting game is not fun, but of course, you know this too. The prison system was created for us to fail. But, if I had anything to do with it, my Babe was not about to be the government's next victim.

I was ready to prove them wrong. Although he was not in prison or the halfway house, he still owed the state five years of parole before he was 100% free and clear. Can you understand the set-up now? The system is no joke, but neither was I. In the meantime, and in-between time, my Babe continued to work the job he hated until he found a new one. He had to. We didn't need any problems with the unknown parole officer. So, the job he hated became a priority for him. You know what they say, do what you must do so that you can do what you want to do. That's "real talk" right there. If you never heard that before, you heard it now.

So far, so good. My man was living up to his word and working on our plan. He is the last of the dying breed *Pho'sho*.

He was working and going to school for his Class A CDL[14] license. Having this trade was creating new opportunities to make more money and have a flexible schedule. I would look at him and be turned on because he learned how to follow the plan vs following his emotions. Just look at what happened for him when he kept his eyes on the prize. He was able to secure a job in transportation to transport the elderly to appointments. He loved this job. He was now able to let go of the job he hated. Did I forget to tell you that he also secured a second job working in a halfway house for a juvenile detention center at night?

---

[14] Commercial Driver's License; Class A is the license to operate commercial tractor-trailers.

EXHIBIT D
THE P/O'S ACTUAL BUSINESS CARD

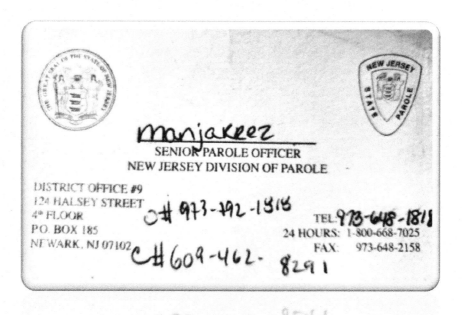

manjakeez

SENIOR PAROLE OFFICER
NEW JERSEY DIVISION OF PAROLE

DISTRICT OFFICE #9
124 HALSEY STREET
4th FLOOR
P.O. BOX 185
NEWARK, NJ 07102

o# 973-792-1918

C# 609-462- 8291

TEL: 973-648-1811
24 HOURS: 1-800-668-7025
FAX: 973-648-2158

SIDEBAR: *He knew not to quit this job until he secured a new one. Lol, Giiiirrrrl, keeping him on task was a tough job, but somebody had to do it. I am so glad he chose me, God, I love him so much. I was more than proud of him; how could I not be? Securing not one but two jobs, he was on a roll. All I could do was say "keep pushing because God has so much more for you." We were more than ready to meet the parole officer.*

PAROLE TIME

We finally got to meet his parole officer (PO). Let me tell you something. Your partner threatens these parole officers. They read their profiles and think that they know everything about these men just from reading a paper. They see all the wrong things they have done and assume the worst about our men. Don't get me wrong, and some have done committed crimes that you should be threatened by. I understand that the PO has a job to do, but at the same time, they have to give a little bit of respect and give them a chance. My Babe's parole officer finally made it to our house. I stood by and observed the PO while I watched my soon to be husband, unable to process what was happening. The fact was this; the PO entered our house (where this man pays the bills and taxes) very aggressively. I wasn't going to allow him to come into our home with his negative energy and demean my man. That wasn't going to happen on my watch. I had to teach my Babe his worth and help him understand that he served his time. Therefore, he should demand respect and not allow anyone to belittle him. These men feel worthless and sometimes want to give up. Not happening. There were rules to the house: no shoes passed the threshold. Surprisingly, this was a problem for the parole officer; he didn't want to take off his shoes. I let him know that he would contaminate our floors by walking in the house with shoes. The PO refused. Here's where the trouble started. I replied that he would have to remove his shoes to enter our house unless he it was written in the parole plan that he didn't have to do so. I continued to say that the same way my husband has to follow the parole rules, the PO has to follow our household rules. I had to argue back and forth with the PO until my message was received. I had to make him understand that everyone was accountable, and in order to wear his shoes in our house, it would have to be included in the New Jersey parole bylaws. Otherwise, those shoes will be removed. POINT BLANK PERIOD!!!! My future husband stood speechless and paranoid, thinking that I was compromising his freedom. However, I was giving him liberty. Your Honor, if you could have seen the look his face. The good thing was, he was processing the situation. You see, in his mind, he was going back to state prison because of me being argumentative. What I needed my Babe to understand was that I wasn't on parole. I wasn't trying to be belligerent, yet I was speaking on his behalf. I knew that he couldn't violate parole just because I was stating the facts. I was setting a tone to ensure he would be respected as a man while on and off parole. This interaction helped him see his new value as a civilian. The PO was there to do a job, get a urine specimen to test for drugs, and make sure he wasn't violating parole. The point was this, if God was able to forgive, who was this man not to? That is why I had to defend my soon to be husband's honor.

Proverbs 13:13 *New International Version (NIV)*
Whoever scorns instruction will pay for it, but whoever respects a command is rewarded.

The PO took off his shoes and began to say, "I will take them off and this time only," and I replied, "If you don't have those bylaws in your hand, you will take your shoes off on your next visit too." On the next visit, we came up with a compromise (you have to work as a team, it's the only way); he wore a pair of shower caps to cover up his shoes. He began to explain, the only reason why he was making a big deal was because he may receive a call for a violation on a different parolee and have to leave abruptly. I let him know that I thank him for giving us the same respect that he was given. We were making progress. He understood our home's rights, and I was happy I didn't surrender to the PO. This proved to my Babe that he had a voice. This changed the game for him, and he was beginning to understand his worth. The barriers were broken, and we began to communicate as equals.

The PO was honest with us. He began to express to my Babe that he never met a woman like me. The PO told him that he was blessed to have me by his side. He continued to share that most of the men who come home don't even have a home to be paroled to. The ones who do, don't even have a bed to sleep in, much less a room. The PO began to look around our home and started pointing out how all his needs and even were met. The PO admired our beautiful, fully furnished bedroom with a king-size bed and noticed that his closet was full of clothes and shoes. The kitchen was fully stocked and the house was nicely decorated. It felt like home; it was welcoming. He let us know that he met tons of criminals and had to always be on guard.

70

He admitted he was nervous after reading Babe's file and was judging him before giving him a chance.

This changed the dynamics of our relationship. Respect is earned, not given, and demanding your respect is a must. It felt great. He was able to do his parole time now with the support of his PO too. It meant everything to me that my soon to be husband had followed my lead and believed in me and my approach. I would have never done anything to hurt him. RESPECT GOES FAR!!!

People have to be taught how to treat you because they don't know unless you teach them. That's a fact. He couldn't allow people from his past to compromise his future. Besides, I wasn't going to stand by and let it happen. We had come too far, and I had sacrificed way too much to allow that to happen. No one would allow him to leave his past life behind. This is something he had to learn; it wasn't going to be easy. The phone calls started, and the knocks on the door began. The hard part was trying to guide him to make the right decisions about the people he interacted with without making him feel like he was being told what to do. Although people were happy to see him, they also had to be taught who he was today. He was no longer Speedy, the street dude, he had evolved into a different man.

One day a few guys came by the house and wanted my him to go out. It wasn't a good look for him, especially while being on parole; I didn't have a good feeling about it either. I told him not to go out with them, and he let me know he could do what he wanted to do. I replied, "If you go out, there will be consequences and repercussions." I continued to say I will call your PO. He left and I made the call. The PO was surprised. He immediately contacted my Babe and told him to meet him at the house ASAP!! When they met up, the PO began to say to him that he was most certain that he had a good woman on his team. Who else would report him without malicious intent? Meeee!! The PO said that my reaching out to me let him know that I genuinely loved him. The PO told him to stay focused and stay on track. He followed up with a compliment and praise for me too. I was told that I was doing a great job and to stay firm, "your soon to be husband is going to need that every step of the way." The PO said that he had great respect for me and my approach. He also told him that he had great respect for him for not being mad and understanding that I was looking out for him. This was growth; this meant that he had to accept that a lot of people, places, and things needed to change in order for him to move forward in life in a positive way.

I could not allow my Babe to deviate from the plan. I had sacrificed so much at this point. He was not the only one locked-up. I was mentally incarcerated. I had to go through a wall, be told what to wear, how to wear it, what time to come in, and what time to leave. I lost a little bit of myself every day because I didn't have anybody to guide me or talk to without judgment. So, I pray that you learn something from me because it's not an easy walk. Parts of the process were more challenging than others, but it can be done with a strategy in place. I thank God that I didn't lose my mind.

Romans 12:2 *New International Version (NIV)*
2 Do not conform to the pattern of this world but be transformed by the renewing of your mind. Then you will be able to test and approve what God's will is—his good, pleasing, and perfect will.

DID SOMEONE SAY WEDDING

We established a good relationship with the parole officer. Babe was working and conquered the goal of obtaining his CDL. What more could a girl ask for? He returned to those streets strong, all because he stayed focused. We agreed on having our wedding ceremony at Maggiano's Little Italy in Bridgewater, NJ. We chose this location because it had a patio with a gazebo behind it and a Marriott hotel directly across the street. Stop thinking nasty! It was so we could have our guests conveniently located. Before I walk you through all the wedding details, let me share with you our last day of being single. I know you think that because he was incarcerated that he didn't have a bachelor's party. That's not true. I knew he would be coming home in September 2008, and we planned to get married on October 19th. So, in that short period of time, I wanted to make sure that he had everything he needed. I wanted to make sure that getting married was something that he wanted to do. So, I hired strippers, and I planned a bachelor party for him. A friend of mine was nice enough to let me use her apartment for the party. Maaaaaaaan, they tore that house up!

Meanwhile, you know me, my mind went crazy just thinking about all the stories about men coming home from prison and just sliding into anything and everything. I was sitting there thinking, "Should I hire these strippers?" "Is he going to sleep with these strippers?" "Is this how he is going to spend his last night single?" Man, my mind was playing tricks on me. Apart from being the "G" that he is, he was loyal and faithful. He didn't engage in any of that from what I know. On the flip side, my bridal party planned a fabulous bachelorette party. I also had a stripper. I really didn't care for the stripper that was chosen for my party, but hey, it was fun. After the bachelorette party, we decided to go to one of the local bars to have a good time. Keep in mind that I don't drink, but I wanted to drink this particular day before the wedding. I wanted to turn up and have a good time. So, I had a few different glasses of liquor, and boy, was I lit! It was a feeling that I never experienced before. My friends called me "Happy Feet" because I danced the night away. Nevertheless, I was still conscious of my surroundings. My Babe taught me to always be aware of what's going on around me. Long story short, my cousin was dancing provocatively, and this guy started to dance really close to her and practically smother her. I watched the guy harass and try to fondle her and she kept telling him no. I said to myself, "He has one more time to touch her, and I'm going to knock his ass out!" Boy, he touched her one more time, and I don't know what came over me, but I knocked him out! It was like a scene from the *Matrix*. His dreadlocks were just flying all over the place. When he hit the floor, all you could see was my bridal party running towards me and taking me out of the bar. I mean, it happened so fast. I bet you he won't fondle another woman without her consent. They called my soon to be husband and said, "You better get over here fast and get her; she just knocked a guy out in the bar!" Maaaan, I don't know where the strength came from, but it sure felt good! It released all of the tension that I had inside of me and all the doubts that I had in my head about getting married.

The morning of the wedding finally came. I was elated. It felt amazing to know that all the time I served, six or six and ½ years, was not in vain, that it wasn't just prison talk, but his true soul speaking to me. He chose me to be his wife! All the girls were scrambling in the halls, and everybody was having a good time making sure that I felt good on my special day. My friends made sure that I had food and everything I needed was taken care of. Having their support meant everything to me. It was so nice to get married and have my family and friends there. Everyone was on the same page. No one treated him like a prisoner. He was welcomed with love and respect as my bridegroom. That meant so much to me. It made my day so much more special. My girls came from all over. My brother's ex-girlfriend even came all the way from Virginia just to do my makeup. I was so happy to see her. She was always there for me and still had my back. I love her to death. You know I can't pick who my brother chooses to be with, but she was one of the good ones that he lost. That's another story. After she finished my makeup, she made sure that I was alright. Then she took her assigned seat at the wedding and awaited my arrival.

Next, my girls came in and took all kinds of crazy pictures. One of my best friends (that already lives in North Carolina) came in the day before the wedding. I believe that every occasion needs a little bit of humor, and she gave us that. I told her to cross her eyes in one of my pictures. So, she made these big ol' crossed eyes for my wedding book pictures. It was so funny.

While I was in my hotel room looking out the window, I saw my brother-in-law riding around the hotel grounds like a big kid in the golf cart I rented to drive me down the aisle. He was the driver and was already having a good time, before I had a chance to ride. THE NERVE OF HIM! I wasn't mad though. He was like a big kid in a candy store.

Once I got dressed, oh my god! The nervousness kicked in. I was so nervous. I started to think, am I going to look nice? Will he think that I'm beautiful? Will he be excited? All kinds of things were running through my head. The butterflies in my stomach were so intense. I just prayed to God to allow everything to work in our favor. God did just that. As I approached the golf cart, my brother-in-law took my hand and helped me into the golf cart. Then we made our way across the street to the wedding venue. I got to the end of the aisle, and I saw my family getting ready to march down the aisle. I didn't do a traditional wedding because it wasn't a traditional marriage. The family marched down the aisle, and we had praise dancers escorted our respective families. The look on my grandmother's face when she saw me was magical. She looked beautiful too. My grandmother's opinion mattered to me above everyone. She is my best friend, my day one. I love my her with my entire heart.

The excitement on everybody's face as I rode down the aisle in the golf cart was priceless. Oh my god, if you could be a fly on the wall and just see the joy and happiness within our space. Wow, it removed any stress and doubt that I had. Keep in mind that we both had eight-year-olds at this time. We made sure that we let our kids be a part of this new union. My son escorted me down the aisle and gave me away. His son was his best man. They were important and we had to validate them, and we did.

As we stood eye to eye exchanging vows, it was the happiest moment of my life. When we finished saying our vows, we were introduced as Mr. and Mrs. to our family and friends. Then, we did the old school ritual. You know, back in the day when there wasn't really a formal wedding, the tradition was to jump over the broom as a symbol of accepting the marriage and solidifying the union. We took that jump! That moment was real! There was no turning back. We were officially husband and wife. It was a ceremony to remember.

We went into the garden and took pictures while the guests went to the reception to have hors d'oeuvres. As they were enjoying themselves, we were outside in the garden having a good time taking picture after picture, after picture, after picture. Oh, my God! If I could have this day one more time. Then we went to the reception hall and waited to be announced by the emcees. My bridesmaids surprised me and put a dance together that amazed me. I was shocked and wondered when they had the time to put the dance together. I mean, everything was so nice! Having the support of everyone that attended our special day made my dream come true and my husband was so happy to see faces in the room that he had not seen in ten years.   Not only was it a wedding, but it was a release party and/or reunion for my husband. Everyone was having so much fun at the wedding that we extended the reception for another hour. It cost us an extra $1,000. That was the most expensive hour of our life, but it was worth every dime. At the end of the day, everyone had a good time, and everyone's support made a big difference. That was all that mattered. It was a great feeling.

THE HONEYMOON

Well, my husband and I had a red-eye flight to catch early in the morning so we could start our honeymoon. But, in the meantime, we made sure that all the tuxedos were collected so the twin could return them to the rental company for us without penalty. We were so tired. I told my husband that he could go home and get some rest, and I'd meet up with him later. He told me no.

Now Ladies and Gentlemen of the jury, this is when you know that there is a big difference between being a girlfriend and being a wife. Usually, he would never give me any problems about running the streets. However, this particular night, man oh man, I knew that the tables had turned. I was no longer his girlfriend; I was his wife. He said, "no, you can't stay here alone." I said, "why not? You usually let me do what I want to do." He said, "that was before I said, "I do," and you became my wife." To understand that I was now his primary responsibility meant everything to me.

We made it back to the house and immediately counted all the money that we collected and then we fell out. There was no more life to us. We didn't get to shower or do anything else but rest. We woke up early to catch our flight to Disney World. Here we are in our thirties, I know a lot of you are saying, "Y'all grown, why are you going to Disney World?" I've been to Disney multiple times, yet he never experienced it. So, it was the best feeling in the world to be able to take my husband somewhere that he had never gone before.

We had food, snacks, and everything that you could imagine. He was like a big kid in a candy store. I knew that I was showing him a bigger world than he was used to. I was helping him expand his mind and didn't even realize it. God was teaching us both and putting us in the right position at the right time. This for me, was a game-changer. It brought tears to my eyes.

Once we arrived in Florida, we picked up our rental car, and we went straight to the hotel to shower. Man, I got dressed up for my husband and put on my lingerie and my stilettos and we fell asleep. In our minds, we had already consummated our marriage. Sex didn't even matter. It was more about enjoying one another lying beside each instead of speaking across a table with others watching. This was definitely a good feeling. The next morning after breakfast we put on our matching outfits and headed over to *Magic Kingdom*. When we arrived, we immediately went to the gift shop and purchased our matching bride and groom hats with the Mickey Ears so we could wear them on the rides. The bride hat had a veil that hung out. It was really, really cute.

All of a sudden, my husband said, "Just put the hat on your head, and let's go." I was so scared, but I did just that, and followed him. I asked what we were doing, and he said that the line was too long. Oh, my God! You can take the man out of the hood, but sometimes you can't take the hood out of the man. LOL! This was so crazy! "What if we get caught?" I asked. He said, "You're my wife now, you can't testify

81

against me." Although this wasn't a good reason, it sure was a thrilling moment.

We went to the municipal courthouse at Disney's City Hall after that. While we were there waiting in line, people came up to us saying "Oh my God, you guys just got married?" Then they said, "Oh my God, you'll regret it." It was so funny. Everybody had a little humor, but they were honest about it. They let us know that the first five years would be the hardest years in our marriage, and boy was that true.

Now I know you all are asking wasn't he on parole? Yes, he was on parole. We took a gamble jumping on a flight and crossing a few state lines. But it was all worth it. We prayed for the covering and safety for our trip. God hears our prayers, so don't judge me. That's what grace and mercy is for.

Your Honor, I wasn't trying to break the law, but men coming home from prison need to have their eyes opened to help them stay on track. This will help them avoid going back to their old ways that sent them to prison in the first place. I hope you will have mercy on me. Anyway, I want the jury to see that they can put their partners in a position to see life from a broader perspective.

WHAT'S BEST FOR THE CHILD

My husband told me he wanted to have five more kids; I told him he had the wrong wife. When he told me God said be fruitful, I replied, "I will give you a piece of fruit, but I'm not in the market of making fruit cocktail." I know y'all rolling on the floor in your mind like me. But I couldn't lie about it, having more children scared me. I had to be truthful with myself and him. I never wanted a whole lot of children. I knew and I understood that. Being born in the hood, the odds of success were against us. I didn't want those pressures on me. I always told myself that if I couldn't provide a safe, positive atmosphere, I would not have any more kids. STOP judging me; I'm entitled to set standards in my life just like you are. I try to live my life in real-time, and the fact that we lived in poverty was real. You see, I have always thought outside the normal scope of people even during my childhood. For that, I was labeled grown but what adults never understood was that I just knew who I was and what I wanted in life from day one. So never minimize the power of a child's mind. Now that we are on the same page, you can understand my thought process a little clearer now. All I wanted to do was to break the cycle of life in the hood. Am I wrong for that? With that being said, I promised my husband at least one child in our union. So, I was committed to one and done.

My husband's son was now coming over and visiting with us often. Once we got married, the pressures were on. My husband and his son's mother wanted the boy to move in right away. The mother was constantly calling demanding that her son move in with us. All the while, I'm losing a piece of myself by the day. Yet, no one saw it because they only saw what they wanted instead of me. I felt like they were pushing me to raise an additional kid that I was mentally and emotionally unprepared for. Now let me explain, my husband knew that he had an obligation to his child, so did I. But he had just completed ten years of prison time, went straight to the re-entry program and then to the halfway house. How could he be whole for his child when he couldn't be whole for himself? I was beyond frustrated because no one would listen to what our reality was yet pointed their fingers to get what they wanted. You guessed it...I became the bad guy.

"REMEMBER TO HOLD ONTO YOURSELF WHILE HOLDING ONTO HIM"

His family bashed me because people were thinking they knew our inside story, NOT! They say, "*assuming will make an ass out of you every time.*" I guess the ASSES shouldn't have assumed my life. I was condemned, but I'm bigger than the people from the outside looking in. Seriously, all I wanted to do was to love and protect the best interest of his child with no interruptions. Let me be very clear, if he was going to be an issue for me, I would have never continued to develop a relationship with him. Can I live a lil' bit? Pleeeease... give credit where credit is due; we had a bond. We were good, so I thought.

I loved this kid from the bottom of my heart from the very start. I loved him like he was my own child. I knew that the healthiest thing to do was to gradually transition him to live with us while his mother maintained a stable environment for him. Was I wrong? We all had to learn each other and relearn how to co-habitat as one unit. My husband and son had the opportunity to rebuild their relationship and gain trust for one another to spark a healthy relationship. This was not an overnight process like people wanted it to be. It had to be gradual so that no one would feel overwhelmed. Besides, my biological son had to go outside the home to visit his dad too. So, what was wrong with his son visiting outside of the home? The mother didn't understand that. Her conversation led me to believe it was a power struggle between my marital relationship and my husband's relationship with his child. She showed signs of hoping for a reconnection with my husband. You know, as women God gave us intuition, we know. This began to cause division, frustration, aggravation, all the "ations" you could think of. It was getting real. However, I had to protect my mind. I had a son to raise too. Was anyone considering that? Nope. The funny part was, if you remember in the beginning of the story, she was allowing him to come over and visit; we were good co-parents (the mother and I) until my husband came home from prison.

You see, everyone had an opinion about how they thought things should have been. But the bottom line is, it was our reality we had to work through. Everybody was not on the same playing field. I thought, how were we supposed to achieve that inner peace to make our blended family work if we couldn't agree? Talking about mentally exhausted. One thing that I have never done is allow anyone to disrupt my peace in my sanctuary, my home. But somehow, it was being ambushed. Home is the one place that I was supposed to be able to let my hair down. What I was going through with my husband was not for the world to see, and it shouldn't have been. I watched him battle PTSD, depression, anxiety, and did I mention the isolation that I had to witness him go through? It was so hard for me to process as an adult. Imagine how a child would process feeling neglected because his dad only wanted to hang out in a room alone and watch movies or play the video game. Although it was not intentional behavior, it was the aftermath of being incarcerated for so many years. This was his new norm, SOLITARY CONFINEMENT! I mean, it was expected; what did they think would happen? Oh, I forgot... No one was thinking about how prison would impact him. I get it though, prison is the way of life in the hood, and no one paid attention to what a healthy recovery looked like since prison life in the hood was normal. Understand me... I only speak facts. Before anybody (in prison or out of prison) can wholeheartedly be there for you or anyone else emotionally, socially, financially, spiritually, they must be whole for themselves. The problem was no one else could see that but me. Was I crazy? I had to have had thick skin to deal with this, and that I did. It took a lot for me to be strong. Dysfunction was on the rise, and I had to protect myself. I had to remember who I was and whose I was. I began to call on God more often. This is the best part about having a relationship with God. No matter how far I may slip away from God, I never forget how to call His name.

NOTE: *Sometimes, people who grow up in dysfunction don't realize the dysfunction when they see it or understand it, for that matter. To be frank, they think that it is normal.*

Here is where I first started to experience what anxiety was. This was all new for me and my husband. Unfortunately, no one got it. This was real, and although he wanted everything to be normal from day one, it didn't happen. It wasn't the hand he was dealt. Not just for him, but for everyone attached to him. Hell, I had to live with him, and his recovery was scary for me because it was unfamiliar territory. I knew that I definitely needed God to overcome this new life I took on. It was a lot for me to keep my husband focused with all the chatter in his ear. I was able to see him in ways that everyone on the outside couldn't see or experience. What about me? I couldn't allow anyone or anything to kill my spirit because I was already feeling less and less of me.

I kept pushing because I saw what endless possibilities, he had to be better than great. He just needed that push and support. I began to say, "Father, give me the strength to continue this journey. Show me my purpose; show me what you want me to do." This may sound crazy to some, but it's true. God began to show me how I would experience rejection, to be talked about, get backlash from my husband and the people on the outside. God showed me how my husband would be overwhelmed and would possibly give up. God said you got this, and I got you, keep walking and don't look back.

Isaiah 45:5 New International Version
5 I am the Lord, and there is no other; apart from me, there is no God. I will strengthen you, though you have not acknowledged me.

FOOTPRINTS

He Spoke, "My Child,
I Love You And Would Never Leave You...
When You Saw Only One Set of FOOTPRINTS, That's
When I Carried You."

-Carolyn Joyce Carty, "Footprints in the Sand,"
(Poem, Quote)

WHAT'S BEST FOR THE CHILD CONT—

His son's mother, family, and friends came at him with the reverse psychology, "you going to let her tell you what to do?" This was normal behavior for those on the outside who are oblivious to prison's aftermath. People, PTSD after prison is real! So instead of becoming the enemy, my husband's ex should've looked at the situation as a glass half full instead of half empty, from one mother to another. Everyone has this idea of how the reconnection works, but are we looking at it as being healthy or unhealthy? That was the question. It wasn't about what we wanted; our collective goal should've been about what was needed for the welfare of the child, my husband's mental health, as well as mine!

Let's be honest, mental health is rarely, (if ever) discussed in a "BLACK FAMILY'S HOME." If this was ever to be mentioned, you were called crazy. So, it was a topic never brought up. For my own mental health, I had a different outlook. My husband was experiencing so many feelings and emotions but didn't know how to express them. Life was deep! However, even with all of this going on, we still had a positive movement going on in our world. This was the beauty behind it all. We never stopped pushing forward; we were in the process of purchasing a house.

MONEY ISN'T EVERYTHING

I managed to overcome the hurdles of teaching him about credit and financial management. We were working our plan or at least trying to. I say trying because New Jersey was where my money was to afford the house we had in our future plan. In his mind, he was set on moving to North Carolina. In my mind, I thought that his thoughts of moving would fade away once he hit the streets. But in fact, when he hit the streets, the conversation about relocating was more frequent. While doing time, we discussed moving into my mother's rental property. However, I was scared of change. Not just scared of change, but was I truly ready to trust him with my entire life? I questioned whether he was mentally, spiritually, and financially strong enough for me to surrender my ENTIRE life too. Keep in mind that I am speaking my truth. I battled with this for some time, and God showed me to keep pressing. I heard him say, "I got you." Although I heard that voice, I can't lie. I asked myself, was that really God, or was my mind playing tricks on me? That same voice shouted out to me... it is ok to relax, you don't have to be the man and the woman anymore. Hmmm... I was moving physically, but mentally and emotionally, I was torn, not to mention the spiritual battle I was having within myself. You think that was something. Keep listening and watch how God put a twist on everything. I'm telling you, if you don't know God, after you finish this, you're going to, or at least I hope you will.

I know you remember the parole officer that I previously spoke about, right? The one that was irate in the beginning, the very aggressive one? You know, the one that didn't want to take his shoes off to come across our threshold? The same one I convinced to give my husband a second chance because he was a good dude? Well, Office Jose Manjarrez was not that irate parole officer he started out to be after all. In fact, he ended up being one of the coolest dudes I met in law enforcement in a long time and becoming our best friend throughout our experience with parole. You see, that house that we were in the process of purchasing, ha-ha...it fell through. In fact, the realtor had a side deal happening with the house, and we ended up losing out on all the money that we put out. Now I know you're wondering how much money, but the money is not the focus. Money was the distraction that God used to align me with the plan, so pay attention. Right after the house fell through for us, Officer Manjarrez was on our team big time. He began to advocate for us in an effort to get my husband's parole transferred to North Carolina. It was him that pulled the trigger for my husband to get that fresh start he was looking for. He fought long and hard for us too. Officer Manjerrez even allowed us a two-week visitation pass so that we could go to North Carolina and get ourselves established. We knew that it would take some time for the transfer to be completed because it was not just New Jersey involved but also North Carolina. The two states had to collaborate for this process to be completed. But the real question was, "how much time was it really going to take?" To that, no one had the answer. We were praying that within those two weeks, we could have the approval completed, wishful thinking. However, it was cool. It turned out to be a very long process, but Officer Manjerrez went to bat for us, and the process went smoothly. I know you're probably scratching your head trying to figure out what changed my mind to move. The answer is simple...GOD, nobody but Him! I knew that he was talking to me. It was no longer about the money, it was no longer about the house, and material things began to lose value to me. God showed me that I had to remove myself from trying to make everything work and allow the order of God's ways to guide me. God said to me just as clear as day, "you have to allow your husband a chance to lead you so that he could become the head of your life." I was trying to understand God's plan as I walked away from everything, trying my best not to look back. Daaaamn... "LOOKING BACK" in my Lauryn Hill voice. I had to allow myself to do the right thing without thought. I had to move. I realized this was the original plan that I forfeited. I had to "BOSS UP[15]" and keep my word solid. I learned that God makes you uncomfortable in life when he is transforming your mind and spirit to take you to new levels of life.

Psalms 56:3 NIV: *New International Version*
When I am afraid, I put my trust in you.

---

[15] Handle your business; Do what you have to do so you can do what you want to do later

THE TWO-WEEK VACATION PASS

The day we got the call that the house was falling through, I made four phone calls. One to my mother to see if her rental property was available, then to my best sister-friend in the Carolinas to see if her husband (my brother) would pack us up because they owned a trucking company. Next to the parole officer to get a pass to travel, and finally, you guess it, to Jesus. I started to challenge those voices I was hearing to see if it was indeed God talking to me. I couldn't stop struggling with the thought about me making such a drastic move in the back of my mind. So, I made a deal with God. I said, "God, if this is you, you will make this transition easy, and everything will fall in place, unlike the purchasing of the house." Now! I know better than to try to make a deal with God (*I pray you to know this too*). God is not a deal maker. But for some reason, I think God was in playing mode. Do you know that every phone call that I placed was a GO! Ok, all I could say is God, you play too much!

SIDEBAR: *God is humorous when you just take a minute to get to know him. I encourage you to read the word of God too; you will see that the current world that is upon us is life repeating itself. God is not new to this, but true to it, true to US!*

It couldn't have gotten any better than that. We were so blessed to have so much love and support. It was like being a part of the Underground Railroad, so to speak. It sounds crazy, but true. We had an entire team of willing bodies that formed an alliance to rescue my husband from bondage. All of these people played a big part in our transition. Their contribution allowed me to be by my husband's side and make sure that he got through the process and made it back to North Carolina.

When the two weeks were over, we needed to head back to New Jersey because my husband's visitation pass expired, and the transfer wasn't completed. We needed a place to stay until the paperwork went through. Not knowing how long it would take, my uncle was generous enough to let us live in his apartment while he stayed with his girlfriend so we could be comfortable while we waited. He never once asked us for a dime, nor did he put a timeframe on us. This is truly what family is about. Once we secured the location, we still had to get it approved. My uncle's house was located in a different county. It was out of my husband's parole jurisdiction, but this was where we had to sleep. The parole officer deemed the environment as being safe for us to stay until the transfer was complete, thank God.

My uncle was a ladies man; he had women everywhere. We would always laugh about how he never had to worry about his brother taking his girlfriends because his niece would take them. I couldn't help that they loved me. I was just a fun person to be around. Needless to say, I formed a special type of bond with most of the women my uncle dated. With some, it was on a business note and some for pleasure. Remember, I did hair, and I also did taxes, so that was always the initial connection. Man, my uncle loved his niece to death, and I loved him even more. He always brought me business because he stayed in the women's face.

I was happy he was a ladies because it worked in my favor. The women may not have liked it, but my pockets sure did. One of my uncle's ex-girlfriend also moved to North Carolina (a few months before me), about two hours from where we were moving to. She trailed us down from Raleigh when we were passing through and came to help us unpack and get situated. When the two weeks were over, I needed someone to be there with my son. Without hesitation, she came to my house and took care of my son. She made sure he was ok. She even took him to the barbershop during a snowstorm. Man, what more could we ask for? Everything was working out; it had to be God. Who else could have been making it all happen that easy? The days went by, and still no word for the approval to transfer the parole.

Meanwhile, God continued to be God and kept showing us favor. I was still able to maintain an income. My clients were coming to my uncle's house to get their hair done. It was tax time, too, so that money was coming in as well. I never missed a beat, making that money. Back in the Carolina's, my uncle's ex-girlfriend and my mother were holding it down for us. The paperwork began to gain traction, and the North Carolina Department of Parole finally reached out. They needed to come and visit the home in which my husband would be residing while finishing up his parole. When the date was scheduled, I notified my mother so that she could prepare to leave work to let the PO in the house for North Carolina's state observation.

Let me give you some background on how that whole process worked. Once the New Jersey parole officer put in the application for parole to be transferred to North Carolina, (the receiving state), needed to approve that the parolee can permanently cross state-lines. Listen to me well... the desired state that the parolee wishes to move to has to approve their stay. The receiving state wants to make sure that the parolee is no threat or a financial burden. Keep in mind, the sacrifice to relocate was real because I had to assume the financial responsibilities for my family in order for the transfer to work. My husband went from having multiple jobs to ZERO jobs. The pressure was on me, and it never once crossed my mind. I was just allowing God to order my footsteps. I never fathomed the hardship that was awaiting our arrival. If I did, do you honestly think I would have moved? NO! This is why the Bible tells us to lean on God's word and not our own understanding. We would never complete the test God prepared for us if we knew what would happen.

Proverbs 3:5-6 New International Version (NIV)
Trust in the Lord with all your heart and lean not on your own understanding; 6 in all your ways submit to him, and he will make your paths straight.

Just when you think you completed your prison sentence, you realize parole is more challenging than being behind bars. The state owns you until you finish the parole time given. It's the setup. They control the parolee's potential ability to grow, hoping to intimidate them enough to give up and fall victim to their old ways. This is why the support system must be on point and have some means of structure, better "ME" than the state. Even though we went down south two weeks before and set the house up, the state could have easily backfired on us and denied my husband's transfer. We could have been homeless. What a gamble I had taken. You see, the state needed to see that I could maintain a safe and secure environment, adequate furniture/bedding, food and most importantly, sustain enough income alone. I then became the main character in the transfer process. Without my financial security, the transfer would have fell through. I had to prove I was financially fit to uphold the welfare of my son, my husband, and myself without a struggle. I also had to prove that I could afford all of our living expenses: i.e., rent, car notes, credit cards, etc. independently. The state knew it was going to be a task for my husband to secure a job and they did not want to assume more tax liabilities. I had to provide bank statements and tax refunds as proof that I could hold it down alone. The parole officer couldn't believe her eyes and began to question my mother. Oh boy! Why did the parole officer feel comfortable enough to do that? My mother immediately went into defense mode for her cub (me). Picture this...

We had moved into a three-bedroom home that I was able to fully furnish with what I already had with still more furniture left in storage. There weren't any empty walls in our new home, not one. The PO asked my mother, how could I afford all this? A fully furnished house and two cars in the driveway. She continued to say that this was unheard of insinuating that I was up to no good. But having a strong mother, she was suited up to give a rebuttal. My mother reminded the PO that she had the requested documentation that verified my income. She further asserted that I always worked hard and for myself. She stated that I had always been a go-getter, doing hair all my life as well as income tax preparation. She ended by telling the PO that she hoped she had provided her peace during the interview. I am sure that PO would not think about questioning my mother again. I hollered when my mother called to tell me. She is not to be played with.

The State of New Jersey

State Parole Board

Termination Certificate

To: ████████████   Inst #: P409925

Address: ████████████████████

Mandatory parole supervision by the Division of Parole is hereby terminated by reason of expiration of the mandatory parole supervision term imposed as a component of sentence pursuant to N.J.S.A.2C:43-7.2.

Given this ____13th____ day of ____September____ 20 11

By: _Julienne Sirico_
Julienne Sirico
Assistant/District Parole Supervisor

Address: PO Box 862
Trenton, NJ 08625-0862

Phone: (609) 943-4431

dts

C: File

Status/Removal Form to be Submitted

LETTER FROM OFFICER

Our recent telephone call took me by complete surprise, but it was a pleasure talking to you about your Husband's re-entry and how his transition has had an impact on your life. It is my pleasure to give you and your readers an overview about my experience and opinion about the parole system. To the prospective reader, my name is Jose Manjarrez. I am a former Parole Officer with the New Jersey Division of Parole, where I was employed from 2004 to 2017. During that time, I supervised many individuals that were under parole supervision including Totisha's current husband. I have since transitioned into a different career. My thoughts, therefore, are personal and are not a representative of that agency.

Although I do not remember every intricate detail of the fore mention's case, I do remember administrating the request to transfer parole to the state of North Carolina and the transfer being approved. In general, persons under parole supervision can request out-of-state transfers through the Office of Interstate Services. At the time, the process included, amongst other things, an application; a case summary; a recommendation; and approval from the receiving state. Structure is important, its interplay with supervision. My memory and experience tell me that structure through family support, financial assistance, counseling services, and general community ties are fundamental for a parolee's success. I am certain that social scientists would be able to give you a much more sophisticated explanation, but I believe that those factors are likely to provide guidance; the means for basic necessities; and the positive pressure of knowing that there are additional stakeholders in the outcome. Conversely, the absence of these types of support mechanisms make re-entry much more difficult requiring the person under supervision to call on his or her own self-determination, which in some cases is missing for a variety of reasons.

It's similarly difficult to talk about parole supervision without mentioning mental health. While not everyone that is under supervision suffers from it; most do. I cannot speak about the topic in its clinical sense but addressing mental health may have a positive impact on a parolee's transition. Consequently, detecting; treating; and monitoring the person's progress in that regard may also determine the outcome of parole supervision. Community supervision can be a tricky endeavor. That is the case for the person under supervision as well as the individuals that do the supervision. There are many factors that play a role in the ultimate results and although my decisions as an Officer were not beyond reproach, it was precisely those imperfections that allowed me to perform my duties in what I believed to be an objective manner. In retrospect, I hope that the good far outweighed the negative.

In closing, I wish you the best of luck and I congratulate you on paying special attention to the topic. Despite having changed careers, parole supervision from the perspective of re-entry and public safety are permanently engrained in my mind. Thank you for your consideration.

Jose L. Manjarrez

NEW BEGINNINGS

The time came. He finally got his approval to make our move to North Carolina permanent. He was ecstatic. He was finally getting an opportunity to have a fresh start, something he never thought was possible. I was happy to be able to get back to my son and a stable environment. It had now hit me; I left everything behind for my husband, including my best friend, my grandmother. It became "His Life, Our Story; I forgot to hold onto me while holding onto him." My reality was real. I sacrificed it all to relocate for the betterment of my husband. It didn't even matter to me because I knew that his reality was the streets, prison, or death. I was not about to have that happen to him when I knew I could help him change his survival probability.

"REMEMBER TO HOLD ONTO YOURSELF WHILE HOLDING ONTO HIM"

Back in the Carolinas is where it all started for me. This is where I became locked up without even knowing what I was going through. I can't express to you enough that mental health is real. Now I was able to speak on it from a personal perspective. Mental health was a forbidden conversation to have growing up. I didn't understand what my husband or I was going through. Your Honor, keep listening to my testimony to understand how what my husband was going through triggered my own onset of depression. When I moved to North Carolina, I had an issue that prevented me from transferring my cosmetology license, and the state of North Carolina wanted me to start all over. Financially, I couldn't afford to do so, and cosmetology was all I knew. I started going out and hitting the road on a daily basis to find a job at a hair salon. I figured it wouldn't be hard. I went from shop to shop, and nothing ever happened. I started getting dark mentally. Doing hair was easy money, and the only thing that I knew how to do to generate a substantial income. It was money in the bank, and it was meeting new people while building relationships. I thought, "What a great way to get acclimated into the Carolinas." This was all I knew, so I thought it had to work out for me. It was my lifestyle. Besides, I would always hear people say, if I could make it in Newark, NJ, I could make it anywhere. You couldn't even imagine how I felt not being able to make my money and live life the way that I knew how. However, God will place people in your life for reasons beyond your own thoughts.

I can remember going to one shop and talking with a young lady who was the shop owner. I was so full of emotion and confusion that I told her my whole story. I had been holding in my feelings because no one honestly understood me. It was like a weight lifted off my chest and talking to a stranger came with no judgment. It was something that I had never done before. By allowing God to guide me, I could sense the Holy Spirit tell me it was ok to speak freely, and I found comfort. Although she did not allow me to work in her salon without my license, she told me about her church home. After not being able to secure me a spot in a shop, I set out to get a job. Talking about foreign, a job was undoubtedly that. All I knew was how to make my own money.

I ended up landing a job selling cars. I never worked for anybody before, so this was different, but it was survival mode for me. Even though selling cars was a long stretch for me, I knew how to hustle. I had game...shit, I was from the hood. I thought selling cars couldn't be that much different. No car sold, no money made. To me, that was the same concept as not doing hair. No customers, no money. It proved to be a cakewalk. Math is a universal language, and I spoke it well. The Cadillac dealership actually had some cool guys that worked there; however, I intimidated them. Why? They weren't used to a challenge. I was a woman, and I had game. They say that selling cars is a man's job. Well, that was before I walked on the scene. In the meantime, back at the house, I would go home to have lunch because the dealership was only minutes away. My husband was home because he couldn't find work. For the first time, his depression was apparent, and I saw the look of defeat all over his face. Most men want to feel like the man of the house and provide. But now the roles were reversed, he was home, and I was out working. I started to notice he would go into deep dark thoughts, and I would ask him, "What's wrong?" It never failed; he would always reply that "I'm ok" when I knew that he wasn't. What was I to do? I couldn't beat it out of him, so I did all I could do at that moment. I just kept going because I had to keep the income coming. After all, if not, my savings would have depleted in no time, and we needed money. I worked at the Cadillac dealership for maybe about two more months. I started getting sick every day, but only when I went to work. What was going on with me? I thought to myself. I began to notice that the unique smell of coffee from a nearby coffee warehouse didn't agree with me. I didn't understand why this coffee was irritating me so much. That was when I found out that I was pregnant, damn morning sickness. Now let's reflect...when I first decided that I would give my husband a baby, it was when he first came home, two years ago. However, from the time he came home, I could never get pregnant. I was discouraged and thinking to myself that the one thing my husband wanted I was struggling to give him. But I remembered clearly that day talking to God and asking him to allow me to get pregnant for my husband. How many of you know that it was in God's timing, not mine? It didn't matter what my situation was in the sight of God. I was just receiving what I prayed for. That was when I truly learned that when you pray to God, you better talk to him in the most intricate details possible because God will give us what we ask for. Sometimes it just may not look like what we wanted. God is faithful; we just fall short in our prayers. We knew that we owed God big time, and we started to search for a church home. We found a church that was about 20 minutes away from our house. We began to fellowship and volunteer. This opened up doors for us to meet new people and become more community oriented. We met some great people and created relationships with other couples. My husband finally had an outlet. He had new friends to play basketball with and could just kick back and have fun with them. It was a pleasure to see him allow new people into his world. God was just getting started with us collectively.

MARK 11:24 NIV New International Version
Therefore I tell you, whatever you ask for in prayer, believe that you have received it, and it will be yours.

Financially, we were spiraling downward, and I didn't know what to do. Never in a million years did I imagine that I would be going through a financial hardship, which was not a part of the plan, or so I thought. I was losing my drive. I started to feel helpless and hopeless. I didn't know what we were going to do. We had to do something and do something quick. I fought through my sickness and continued to work selling cars a little bit longer. When I would show up at home for lunch, my husband would be so happy to see me. Although he couldn't find a job, he was hopeful because God planted this baby in me for him. It was the funniest thing to me because my husband had the symptoms of a pregnant woman. My husband would sleep in the middle of the day and just be overly exhausted. Besides the smell of the coffee, I was good. On the other hand, he became the mother hen of the house. He would watch his stories while making sure everything was in place. He washed clothes, dried them, and folded them. Now! This was something I could get used to. He still wouldn't cook, but that was cool, because I love to cook. To me, food always brought people together. So this worked out for a while, but as the weeks went by, it got even more challenging for me to cope with the coffee's smell. It was grossing me out. I eventually quit my job selling cars. My husband is the last of the dying breed; he couldn't allow us not to have any income coming in. I often craved McDoubles, fries, and pizza. So my husband decided that he was going to work at McDonald's. Remember the church we started attending? One of the members owned a pizzeria, and they needed help. They hired my husband on the spot. He was now able to fulfill my cravings. He didn't stop there; he even applied for food stamps setting his ego aside to make sure we were ok. Now that is what you call a real "G." Damn, I love him.

He was determined to work some type of job until something better came up. I love the beauty of networking. Being home allowed me the mindset to create an action plan to move our family forward. This baby was coming, whether we were ready or not. I ended up reaching out to an old friend from high school. He had been working for Pepsi for some time and had a little clout. I asked him if he could help my husband with getting a job, and without hesitation, he said yes. My husband did everything he was supposed to do to get the job. Not just any job, but a job that he could be proud of. God is good. You see, coming home from prison and getting a job is not easy, but moving to another state with a record is much more demanding. I was beyond happy for him. We were not out of the woods yet; he still had to work two weeks in the hole before he would receive his first paycheck. It was still the process that he had to go through. We were coasting.

BABY LIFE

My stomach started getting bigger; she was commencing to take over me. My husband was at Pepsi and working long hours. But at least he was working, and we were grateful. Remember the General Hospital soap opera I told you he would watch? He had me watching it through my pregnancy. Up until this point, I had never watched the stories a day in my life. I was turned out. I would watch General Hospital every day just like he used to do, and that's where we got the name, Callie. She was his favorite character; he would say she is feisty like me. We decided that if I had a girl, she would be named Callie.

Struggling trying to get back on our feet, we still had financial obligations that could not be broken. Once you sign a contract, you are committed until the end of the term. So financially, we were barely making it in a house of three and a baby on the way. His baby mother found out I was pregnant and said because I was no longer just his wife and was about to become his baby mother too, she stated she was going to file for child support. This was the dumbest crap I ever heard of. I had to let her know that I would never be his baby mother. I would only be his wife with a baby, big difference. She didn't like that at all, and I guess it honestly sunk in that the boy is mine in my Monica and Brandy's voice. You have to know music to catch that.

We had two car loans, car insurance, rent, and credit cards that we were living off to make our ends meet. Because of her spitefulness, we had to figure out

110

how to meet all those obligations after the support started. Boy, how much more could I take? I kept asking God what He was trying to show me or if I was being punished? Either way, it didn't feel good at all. I was broken. I always tried to do right by people, yet I was receiving the shit end of the stick. Maaaaan times got hard, and I was stressed out for the duration of my pregnancy.

I know a lot of you are saying, "at least we were living in my mother's house." NOT! My mother wanted her rent money and played no games about it. I needed my mother to be my mother, but she would only come as the landlord. I needed some relief from somewhere, but the relief never came. Why? Because everyone knew I was strong and always made it happen. No one heard my cry for help; no one would lend me a lifesaver, yet they watched me drown. It felt like every man for themselves. Could this be really happening? I sowed enough seed, yet I couldn't reap any harvest.

The day after having my baby on December 3, 2010, I went into postpartum depression almost overnight. It wasn't hard to do being that I was already in a dark place. What was supposed to be a joyous occasion just pushed me deeper into depression. On that day, it started with my mother calling me at the hospital asking for the rent that we did not have. The conversation turned ugly, very fast, because I was hurt. I knew we needed to pay rent, but my mother also knew we didn't have it. She also knew my husband just started working a few months before I gave birth and that we were facing a child support case. Not that those were her problems, but I needed my mother's support, not a landlord. The conversation was so volatile that the nurses on duty ambushed my room thinking that my husband was laying hands on me. But it was only me crying in anguish for my mother. The nurses were trying to calm me down and snatched the phone from my hands and hung it up. They were trying to connect me with a social worker, but I refused the help. I just thought it was something I could get through on my own. Seconds later, it was time for our phone conference with the court's child support division. This was all on the same day. Damn, I wanted to come up for air, but it was like someone was holding my head under water to drown me intentionally. We had to get the nurse to fax over the paperwork that provided proof of my husband's income. The courts said that my newborn daughter was not a part of the child support claim because I didn't have a job. He also stated that it was my fault if I didn't work and not his. Could he have been any ruder? People never know what someone else is going through, and this judge could have really tipped me over to the point of never coming back, but God allowed me to have this baby, which gave me the strength I needed. My son was already good, even though I knew I had to be there for him just the same, he was strong like me, and he resilient.

Nonetheless, even though my child needed support, she was not included in the case. All proceeds went to this one child who was 14 years old.

We were left to live off of a $200.00 a week paycheck. Yup, you heard right, $200.00 a week. All I could do was pray that the tax season would hurry up so that I could make some money again. I prayed, Lord, just let us make it to January.

We all know that life is not set up fair. We also lost the food stamps because my husband had an income, go figure. The food stamp office is like every other agency, only concerned with the gross and nothing else. They didn't care about the child support that left us hungry. What was next? I asked. It was happening so fast that it was the new normal for us. We never knew what was next or when, but we did know something terrible was lurking, and boy, were we right. If you knew me, it was easy to see that there was something going on with me. Yet, no one was paying attention. I no longer had my fire, and that animated spirit was gone too. I was just living one day at a time, that was all I knew how to do. Who am I? I would ask myself. In the meantime, God was teaching me about who I am or, better yet, whose I am. It's still so surreal to me. Each obstacle became more challenging for me to handle and I forgot to hold onto me while holding onto him.

Initially, my mother-in-law was supposed to help me with the baby. However, she was unable to make it due to medical reasons. But I wasn't left alone. One of my best friends flew to North Carolina from New Jersey to take care of me right after I had the baby. That was a good feeling to know that even in my distance, I was still loved. Everything was good while she was there. It was like God blocked anything and everything from

113

happening while she was with me. I didn't want her to leave; the energy she brought to me was breathtaking. She had a baby herself six months before me. She and the baby came, and she took baby Callie, so that I could get some rest mentally and physically. She cooked, cleaned, and made sure my womb was taken care of because I had a Cesarean birth; I mean, she was there for me and my family. I will forever love her for that. This meant everything to me, and I owe her my life. Shortly after she left, the buffoonery started again.

GOD HAS A BIGGER PLAN

The bank even came to repossess my vehicle. Thank God I knew how to read and write. The final document that was mailed to my home stated that I had ten business days to make an arrangement. To that end, it was only the third business day at that point. When I called the credit union to notify them that they had made a mistake, they told me that I needed to fax them over a copy of the letter in order for them to consider releasing my vehicle back to me, as if they didn't have their own copy. Usually, I would throw all the mail in the garbage because the thought of the bills would trigger my anxiety. On this particular day, I heard God's voice just as clear. He said go look in the mail drawer. I thought I was going crazy. But it was really God speaking to me because when I went to the drawer, there was the letter right before my very eyes. The rest was history. They had to release the car back into my possession immediately at no cost. I wanted to push the envelope even more and make them bring it to me. However, I opted not to. One of my church members was at my house and offered me a ride to pick up my car. You can't tell me that God is not real. He is so good to me. Through all of the obstacles we encountered, God always showed us favor every time we were ready to give up. On this journey of darkness, God kept revealing himself to us. God kept showing me how to lean on Him and not my own understanding.

PROVERBS 3:5-6 NIV New International Version;
*Trust in the Lord with all your heart and lean not on your own
understanding; in all your ways submit to him, and he will make
your paths straight.*

But let me tell you that I have always accepted God and always praised Him even in my storms. I was at a place in my life where God was my absolute first priority. I knew there had to be a blessing in all this adversity, but when? Let me be clear, I never stopped acknowledging Him, but we praise and worship the way that we should have either. God is one of a kind, even though I may not have deserved it, He always seemed to show me favor. What an awesome God He is. I only had four more business days to set up an arrangement on my car before they repossessed it. And this time I may not have gotten it back...but God. On the seventh day, God turned this dire situation into greatness. That final day I checked the mail only to find a check with my name on it for ten thousand dollars. Yeeeeessssss! Ten thousand dollars. A check that I had completely forgotten about that I had in New Jersey. Some years ago, before I moved, I was in a minor accident. The lawyer had settled but didn't have my forwarding address. I guess God helped him out. God is never late but always on time. I was able to bring my payments up to date and keep my car. If I had any doubt roaming in the back of my mind, God surely removed it that day. I was ready to learn whatever God was trying to teach for real now; this was nobody but GOD!

THE SHOP

On top of my postpartum depression and all the other darkness I was dealing with, I could not take anymore. I told my husband that I needed to get that drive back in me. I needed to feel something because I was so distraught. I did not recognize the person I was anymore. Who was she? Who was this imposter taking over me? We were struggling financially and going through it. One day my daughter decided to tell me that she wanted her nails done. She was about two years old. I was like, ok. We started to paint our fingernails and toenails. That was our mommy and daughter bonding time. We would have snacks and do all the cute, girly stuff. We enjoyed it and had a great time doing so. A bright light went off in my mind. "How many other children want their nails done?" "This would be awesome!" The adrenaline began to race through my body all over again.

My husband suggested that we go out to get breakfast. I looked at him and thought, "we can't even afford breakfast." Since he asked me to go, I decided not to hurt his feelings. During breakfast, my mind was racing. I still had those little hands and feet in my head. I also wondered how many other little girls would like to get their fingers and toes painted. After we had breakfast, I let my husband know that I wanted to test drive a new car. Every few years, I always replaced my current car with a new vehicle. I could not do this for some time because of the financial hardships we were going through.

This particular day we decided to go to the Honda dealership near where we were. I never test drove a Honda before. I always loved foreign and luxury cars, that was my thing. I felt buying luxury cars was a symbol of my success and I deserved to treat myself to something nice. This was my mental process. I didn't need to buy a basic car. That was how I justified purchasing large or expensive vehicles. It brought me satisfaction and was one of my vices. Everybody has their own vices, so don't judge me. When we went into the dealership, they asked me for my driver's license, and I knew that they were going to run my horrible.

We moved to North Carolina with a credit score of over 700 to end up with a 400 credit score. Who would have ever thought? My credit was never that low, but it is what it is. The car dealer allowed us to test drive this Honda and wanted us to get this deal. They did everything possible for us to be approved for the loan. A credit score of 400, you heard me right. How in the hell could the dealer come back and approve me for a $30k loan? This is when I knew that God was still talking to me. After I test drove the car, I asked the dealer, "How did I get approved for the loan?" The dealer said that even though your credit score is low, your payment history shows that you always paid your car note on time. You have good car credit, so despite it all, they overlooked everything and saw the greatness. That, to me, was an indication of God showing me that there was still something great for me.

Even though the midst of the storm. It may sound crazy to you, but it made a whole lot of sense to me.

With that, I was able to tell the salesman that it sounded, good, but I needed to talk to Jesus and see whether or not this was a blessing or a curse. God gives blessings, and the devil gives gifts. Sometimes it can become dressed in the same way. I needed to know that this was real. Keep in mind that we still had two vehicles at home. One that I just paid off (which was my husband's car), with the money I earned while filing income tax returns for my clients. Now we have a car with a title in hand that we own outright and another car that we were financing. It wasn't much more that we had left to finance on the vehicle. It happened to be a Mercedes SUV that we almost paid off. We were going to make it work for us one way or another. I know you're wondering why we were out looking at another car? This is why I had to go into prayer.

Let me just finish because it gets good how God works. I went to the salesperson and asked him to give me 24 hours to make a decision. We all know how aggressive car salesmen can be. He did not give me 24 hours to make my decision. Instead, he kept calling me on my part-time job. At that time, I was working at the hospital, and I hated this job, but I was working it out to satisfy my husband and my mother. They felt that you needed a "9 to 5" to have legitimate employment. That's a whole other story. Since the salesman did not respect my time frame to make a decision, I began to research different vehicles that I could purchase with the approved loan.

I saw that there was a particular vehicle that I liked located in another town. I'm still a "hustler." I'm still a "G."

My mind started kicking in. I called the car dealership back and asked the salesman what bank approved me for the loan? When he released the information to me, you guessed it. I took the loan to another dealership. The one thing about me is that respect means a lot and goes very far with me. The car salesman did not respect the time that I asked to be in prayer. I needed to make sure that it was the right decision before I stepped out with no money, no down payment just to get a car, and into debt. At the end of the day, I knew only God could remove all of these different finances and any obstacles to prevent this from happening. Who goes into a dealership with a 400 credit score and gets approved for a $30k loan? God started talking to me even more.

We picked up the new vehicle. My husband allowed me to sell the car that we paid off. When I sold the car, I saw a little house in the area that looked like a little dollhouse. When we first moved to North Carolina, I saw this house and said, "I love this house!" "I can make it into a hair salon; it's adorable." I thought it would be so nice for women to come in and just feel beautiful. Unfortunately, the place was never available. The day that I decided to step out of the house, my husband asked me where I was going? I told him that I was going to start a business. He said to me that he knew I was up to something, so he was going to fall back and let me do my thing. This was when this certain house became available. What were the odds of that? I started to tune in to what God was coaching and revealing to me.

Well, I went back and forth into this house, and finally, the owner of the house asked me what I wanted to do with the space. I told him that I wanted to turn it into a kid's spa. Although I was not a hairstylist, it still fell into the cosmetology field. I was able to do what I loved and market it for entertainment purposes only. Therefore, I didn't need a cosmetology license to operate the business. I didn't use chemicals or any tools to cut or draw blood from kids just to have fun. It turned into an idea that manifested into something extraordinary. It was not only a blessing for me or our finances; it was also a blessing for the community. God started to open more doors. The landlord of the place decided to help me out. He said that he didn't understand why he had to help me out. I knew that he would help me out because God had already mandated him to do so. Wow, God is so amazing! I said, "I hear you, God." I was blessed by the landlord splitting half of the rent with me for a whole year until I was able to get on my feet. All I could think about was that I am moving my family forward, and it didn't stop there. I began to start pouring and crying out to God to amend my prayer. I asked Him for a place of business but forgot to add the intricate details.

Remember, in the beginning of the book, I stated that you must pray in intricate details for God to truly understand the core of what you are looking for. So, I had to go back and amend my prayer. My prayer was, "Lord, I need what I need to put in it, do the fingernails, little toes and give parties." God allowed that to happen. I went to various sites (Craigslist, etc.) to get what was needed for the business. I lucked upon a tattoo parlor that was going out of business. The owner of the company practically gave me whatever I needed for free and delivered it to me. That was nobody but God's work. So, now we have the building for half price, the furniture that I needed also for half price. What about the interior? How was I going to afford the interior for the business? I was running out of money, and didn't know what I was going to do. God let me know that my husband was still the head of the household, and he had my back. This is what allowed me to see that my struggle was not in vain with my husband's recovery.

God showed me through the trials and errors that he was learning. As we were working in the shop, the guys came to give me a price to paint. Usually, my mouth is just loose. This particular day God yielded my mouth and told me to be quiet. Then my husband spoke and said, "How much?" Then he said that he would take care of it. I'm looking at him like, where did you get money from? He really made my day. He said to me that he knew that I would go out here and start a business, and I was waiting for you to say something. He had money saved in a pension that he had. Remember the job that my friend helped him get at Pepsi? That's where he earned the money to give me to start my business. I felt good. I no longer felt as though I was making things happen by myself. To have his support and know that he loved me that much to help get my drive back and was prepared for the outcome was a big deal to me. This was really, really good.

The business was now in fruition. Everyone in the community was happy. I had customers coming from the beginning and end of North and South Carolina to visit my kid's spa. It was amazing to see how God allowed the blessing of this one idea from quality time with my 2-year-old daughter and the roadblocks of not being able to get my cosmetology license to manifest. The moral of this chapter is that no matter what, God will make a way. God blessed me with a new car and a way to make the car note payments through the business that I was also blessed with. God revealed to my husband and I to work as a team and to work as one. When we came to work in one accord, God allowed us to move and continue to be blessed. Our finances were starting to improve. Even though our sons were not living with us, and we missed the bonding relationship that we had with them, God allowed us to stay on task and not lose focus. We had to recover spiritually, emotionally, and financially. God was still working on us. The business remained open for over five years, and it was a success. Unfortunately, we had to close the business because there was infrastructure work being done to revitalize the area and expand the highway. As a result, the traffic would back up for miles to come. Unfortunately for me, it impeded customers' ability to locate us and commute to the shop. Overall, the business was a real success, and it spearheaded where we needed to be financially. God is good. In the interim of all these things happening, I never forgot who

God was. Being obedient was the true meaning of my transformation. It also showed me the true meaning of why we relocated to North Carolina. I didn't relocate because of my husband, as I initially thought. God showed me that I relocated to lean more on him and not my own understanding. GOD IS GREAT!!!

PARENT VS. FRIEND

My husband and I would always argue about his son moving in with us. He would rather be friends than a parent who disciplined his son. I finally gave in and said let him come because I was sick and tired of hearing the same thing over and over. That was not fair to me. My husband was a truck driver and was never home, so what quality time was he going to give? Whose responsibility was it going to become?...mine and I wasn't in the mental space for the challenge. I mean, it was hard trying to maintain it for my own children. For the life of me, no one heard me crying out. I was mentally tapped out. I was stressed and depressed, but I had to take care of my kids because I had no other choice. I did not need any extra pressure on my plate. I was honest and truthful to myself and his parents. It was a selfish act of the mother and the father. The mother just was on the outside looking in, assuming the life we lived was perfect without understanding the darkness in which we lived daily. As far as my husband, he was just living in his guilt for being absent. Neither one of them cared about what was best for my son from another mother. They both had a point to prove. The funny part was that they wanted to prove it to the wrong person. Why would a mother make it seem like my husband was choosing me over the son? That was not right. Instead of always reaching out to argue, her ears should have been pierced to hear my voice. But the reality was it's all in the maturity of the mind, and apparently she wasn't there yet, and neither was my husband. Let me talk some real talk to you. There could never be a choice between a spouse and a child. The way that a man loves his partner (a connection that triggers the mind, body and spirit) is totally different from the love between a parent and a child. The intimacy between a husband and a wife is different, so it wasn't about choosing. It was about what was healthy for the child. I had two children that I already had living in my darkness, and I didn't like it for them. So why would I want that for someone else's child? I was feeling guilty enough. Damn, now I was the mean old stepmom. I felt like I was on a hamster's wheel, and I could not get off. All I could think about was how selfish these parents were? His mom and I began to open the lines of communication, doing what we thought was best for the child. We finally agreed that he would move down to North Carolina.

He was 15 then. Although we were not where we needed to be financially, we were moving closer. So we decided to make it work and allow my son from another mother to see that everything wasn't green on the other side. I realized that the bond between his mother would never be broken, but he also had to have some form of respect for me. The respect for me didn't just apply to him, but to my son too. These are all the things that he had to learn. So, yes, you guessed it. I had to be the mean stepmom, and my husband got to be his friend. This is part of the reason why I never wanted him to move in. They needed us as parents, especially as teenagers. I knew the kids would love us for it in the long run. You must have boundaries. It began to be overwhelming for me, but I said I was going to do it. The mom later admitted that she filed for child support out of spite. As a result, the court ordered for the monies to be garnished from our joint tax return. The guilt or conviction was eating at her, so she said that when her child moved down to North Carolina in September, she would return the tax money that had been taken from us. I agreed and also said to her that I'm a bigger person than that, and since she had him for almost half of the year, we could do 50/50 on the tax return. He would then begin to be with us for the duration of the year. I thought that was fair because him moving with us was now an expense.

We sacrificed our family room so that the kids could have a place to stay and not be tight or on top of one another. We wanted to make sure that they had a place that they could call their own. A place where they could be free, have fun and bond with one another. This was something that they already enjoyed doing. So, I wound up making the family room into the boys' dormitory, so to speak. It was really cute. They had wall units filled with their clothes and extra blankets since the room got very cold because it was not insulated. I emphasized to the mom that since she was sending back half of the tax return, I could get the boy's room insulated before the winter months, so we didn't have to use heaters. And we didn't want to do that because it would be a fire hazard. She agreed she would send the money, and we would move forward. The movement started, and my stepson arrived. I made sure that I included her in pictures and allowed her to see the environment that her child was going to be in. It was only fair, as a mother, I understood. I wanted her to feel included, without violating my sanctuary.

Once the child arrived, he wanted to do his own thing. I had to become the "bad parent" because he started teaching my son how to bring girls into the house and how to sneak out at night. These were things that I was not mentally strong enough to handle at the time. Keep in mind that my husband was away driving over the road. And when he was home, he would be uninvolved with the parenting and would just chill-ax[16]. It became my responsibility, which was the second reason I did not want to allow the child to move in. Mentally, you must be able to handle teenagers' behaviors or a child of any age for that matter. Then of course, the way someone else raises a child will be different from your upbringing. So, these were things that I was not ready to introduce my child to. I knew that it would become a negative factor because they were teenagers, and they will try you. I was at the breaking point to expose his deceitful behavior to prove my point. Mentally, my husband did not process the fact that I was not ready to take on this troubling responsibility. Again, we're back to what we want and when we want. If you're not mentally ready to be a parent and discipline inappropriate behavior, it doesn't work. We all have to do our part as parents. Due to the guilt of being incarcerated, my husband never wanted to reprimand his son, so it became my battle. And his took advantage of his guilt and basically felt he could

---

[16] Relax without a care in the world

do whatever he wanted to do. Well, what did that do to my child? I had to deal with the repercussions of this behavior, which was very hard on me. Any who, we decided to jump in the car and drive to Atlanta, GA. At three, my daughter was getting invitations to modeling agencies. We decided to jump in the car and drive to Atlanta. During that trip, my son from another mother and I began to bond again. Things seemed to get better. We were bonding as a family. Unfortunately, there is always something that will tear you down, and Lord knows it did. It happened at the wrong time. I happened to be out with the boys, and we were discussing their upcoming 16th birthdays since they're only two weeks apart. Even though my finances were not stable, I was able to accommodate the boys with what they wanted for their birthdays because I had great connections. While planning their birthdays, we were out shopping, and my son from another mother accompanied me into the various stores. This was something he enjoyed doing with me.

When we arrived back to the car, there was an argument transpiring on the phone between my husband and his son's mother. She was not going to send the money that we agreed upon per her son moving in. This was just a slap in our face because, financially, we couldn't afford to insulate the boy's room. I felt that she was out of line because:

1. She proposed (*sounded good at the time*) that she would send the tax return money back to us because she felt bad.

2. We agreed on her sending only half *(trying to be fair)* of the tax return money, so the boy's room could be insulated.

We didn't want the money for ourselves. We wanted to make sure the kid's room was up to code to fight the cold. When she forfeited, I got on the phone to try to talk to her. She became very irate, calling me out my name and calling me all kinds of bitches. I responded by calling her a bitch. My son from another mother decided to join in the conversation to disrespect me and call me a bitch too. That was the breaking point to let my husband and I know that this was not going to work. His son could no longer stay in our home because he does not have the right to disrespect me. I told my husband that I need his son to pack his things because he can no longer stay in our home. His son responded back to me that he was not going anywhere because he was staying in his father's house. I told him that I didn't care whose house it was. We are united as one, and this was the household that we ran together. Bottom line, his son does not have the right to be disrespectful to me. Therefore, he had to leave. This was something that my husband and I discussed prior to him moving into our home. If the disrespect became overwhelming, I would make arrangements to return him to his mother. At that point, my son from another mother assumed that the phone was disconnected, but the phone was still linked. My husband actually heard him speak these disrespectful words to me. In response, my husband let his son know that he had to leave because the disrespect was not going to be tolerated. Everything that my husband refused to believe, he was now able to see for himself. The guilt ran deep for his son.

I was so grateful that he was able to man up and not allow me to be the bad guy alone within this situation. I also witnessed him antagonizing my son to the point of wanting to physically fight him. It was like he had so much anger and animosity towards him. This was also a situation that I was not mentally prepared to deal with. It was like my stepson's mother threw a monkey wrench in our familial relationship to purposely destroy it. As an end result, I purchased a train ticket for my stepson and informed his mother when he would be arriving at the train station for her to pick him up. When we arrived back home, and the anger had dissolved, he assumed that everything was ok and he didn't have to leave. What he failed to realize was that the damage was already done. I explained to him that he could always come to visit even though he could no longer live with us. He also could keep his North Carolina address for college and financial purposes since it was already established for him. I wanted him to know that I would be there for him no matter what the circumstances were and wanted him to excel. The aftermath of him leaving our home was that my son began to have the same negative energy. What I did not want to happen became my reality. My son continued to sneak out of the house and became disrespectful by talking back to me. These were things that I didn't experience before, but now had to deal with. I didn't have a choice. But God gave me the strength to realize that the rules not only applied to my son from another mother, but also to my son. Thank God for the Word of God that commands us to honor thy mother and thy father, so our days shall be longer. Scripture is everything; scripture was all that I had to rely on throughout all of these heartbreaking scenarios in my life. So when I looked at the Word of God, it allowed me to understand that I could release him too. I had to show my husband that my word was my bond[17]. I got in contact with my son's father to let him know that I raised our son as far as I could and needed to release him because the disrespect could not continue in my house. Although I did not put him on the streets, he had to go where his father was, which meant back in the hood. This was everything that we were trying to avoid; yet, he caused me to make a decision to release him back into the hood. All I could do was pray about it. Now I have a son in the hood, a son that was disrespectful to me, a child that we agreed to move into my house who disrespected me that contaminated my parenting. How do I feel? It was a lot to weigh, but I had to go through it, and it made sense. I sheltered myself. Now I pondered on whether or not he had the tools and skills to understand the hustle and game when it came his way. Maybe it was for a good reason for him to leave. Maybe he needed to learn the hard way. It was a thought that ran through my mind

---

[17] trustworthy

every night, "Is my son, ok?" "Will he be ok?" These were all the things that everyone had judgment about. No one understood the core and the heart of what was really transpiring in my world or within my mental state of mind; and in my husband's mental state of mind. Again, the same amount of time it takes to go to prison is the same amount of time it takes to recover once out of prison. It all depends on when the individual allows the recovery to be a priority or when they decide to even acknowledge the fact that they need to recover. That's when the healing begins, and we were not there yet.

We were now at home with just our little girl. We went from two sons living with us to having none. How do I recover from that? It was hard, but I loved both of the boys and always wished them nothing but greatness. However, what would the outcome be? As a parent, I had to walk around with a feeling of failure because I allowed my husband's actions to compromise our children's destiny. People don't look at the reality of where it all began. It began when my husband made the decision that led him to prison. His guilt prevented him from parenting and disciplining his child accordingly. Ladies and Gentlemen of the jury, pay attention; everyone in the story plays a part. Unless everyone is on one accord, it will never work.

HOSPITAL

Eventually, all of that stress landed me in the hospital. One day while at work, my manager asked if anyone wanted to go home because the schedule was overstaffed. Naturally, I replied: ME without hesitation. I was mentally tired, and my body was shaking. I just attributed the shaking to my allergies and asthma. I had just used my asthma pump, and that type of medicine made me jittery sometimes, so I thought nothing about it. Once I was set to leave work, I didn't even call my husband. I needed a mental break from him too. I called my mother (because she lives closest to the job) and told her that I was tired and was coming over to her house to sleep until it was my actual time to clock out. It was all planned so that I could go home at my regular time. I didn't want anybody to bother me anymore. I just wanted peace for a minute. When I got to my mother's house, she fixed me a plate and said:

MOTHER: "Daughter, you don't look good, and I'm feeling some type of way."

ME: "What do you mean I don't look good?"

I'm looking at my mother like that was so disrespectful. I'm full of jokes most of the time, but she was serious and got the blood pressure machine to check my pressure. When my mother checked my pressure, it was 300/200. Yeah, you heard me right 300/200. I was a stroke waiting to happen. God never left my side, do you hear me?

At that point, I called my husband to let him know what was going on and to look out for me because I was coming home first. Still putting everyone first, I immediately knew that when I went to the hospital, they were going to keep me. I know you're going to think I am crazy, and sometimes I am... I went home and tried to cook a meal so that my family could have food to eat and prepare the clothes for school and work for everyone. I was still trying to be their superwoman.

"REMEMBER TO HOLD ONTO YOURSELF WHILE HOLDING ONTO HIM"

Finally, I went to the standalone ER; it's literally an emergency room without a hospital attached. They immediately rushed me to the back to give me medicine to bring the blood pressure down at check-in. However, the medicine they gave me made me fall asleep. When I woke up, I saw everyone around me, including my husband and the doctors, asking me questions like "Do you know where you are?" Always sarcastic, I replied, "...in North Carolina, all the hospitals look alike, so I know I'm in one of them." At that point, I didn't realize that I was transferred to the closest hospital, and I had been asleep for three days. The doctor explained that they had been trying to bring my pressure down without success. I knew I was overly consumed with stress, depression and anxiety. I was overworked, underpaid, overthinking, and misunderstood. In the back of my mind, I kept sharing with everybody, that life was all too much for me. If they didn't believe me before, I guess it was real now. I guess my body couldn't take it anymore. This was when I really learned that God was keeping me! He didn't allow me to stroke-out. He just wanted my attention to sit down. God would do things like that to me all the time, but not quite like this. This was a decade of walking with God. It was a way that I had never walked with him before. This time it felt different. I was in a situation where God forced me to apply his word into my life. However, I was still not 100% out of the woods. My pressure was still high. I was at a space in my life where I was acknowledging Him in the way that He wanted me to. I was not worrying about what people thought or what people felt about me anymore. I was at a turning point. All I needed to do was understand what God needed from me. That was the only validation I needed. The doctor told me that I would be transferred to the main campus (where I worked) and placed into ICU because he could not get my blood pressure under control. The funny part was, all of my paperwork kept coming back, indicating that I was strong and healthy; this was pissing the doctors off.

Once I arrived at the trauma center, they stuck needles down my throat and in my neck. I remember complaining that I wasn't a test dummy. I asked why the doctors couldn't figure out what was wrong with me despite all the tests. These doctors thought I was going to take their career to the next level if they could only figure out what's going on. I kept hearing the doctors whisper, "why didn't she stroke out, why didn't she go into a coma?" why didn't she have a heart attack?" All I could do was laugh on the inside because I knew God was keeping me. I didn't do any of those things because I had a purpose God needed me to live through.

I realized that no matter what people say or what people thought, I was different. God was showing me that I was on a mission that he placed me on and the only thing that mattered was that I followed His Word. Still, in the trauma unit, I was literally admitted to a room on the same floor of the department I worked for, and no one I worked with came to visit me. That's when I knew that my purpose was not to work for anyone. I mean, I've always known that, but this just gave me confirmation that I was doing was God was asking of me. It was time to stop allowing everyone, including my mother and my husband, to convince me to work for anyone. God was proving to me that He gave me the tools I needed to be successful, I just had to activate them. Needless to say, the doctors were truly upset because they could not figure out what was going on with this healthy African-American woman with a pressure of 300/200. But, all they had to do was ask me.

After five days being hospitalized, I knew the doctors wanted to say that I had lost my mind and that I was crazy, but of course, they didn't use those words. There was about eight or nine people in my hospital room, including my mother. The moment the doctor looked her way to get her input, I intercepted before my mother could utter a word. I love my mother, but her opinion didn't matter because God had already shown me what was wrong with me. No! I wasn't crazy, that would have been easy for the doctors to diagnose. I was able to tell the doctor exactly what was wrong with me. It was the same thing that I told my husband, my husband's child's mother, my children, my family, and my friends. I was simply overwhelmed with life. I had anxiety, stress, and was depressed. I was in a war of worlds and didn't understand the life that I was living or who I was living it with. I was working a job that made me feel worthless and robotic. I was unappreciated working for minimum wage, in school full-time, and running a brick-and-mortar business. I was raising a toddler and a disrespectful teenager, dealing with my husband's emotional battles, PTSD, stress, and his nightmares. All that was wrong with me, I carried on my shoulders alone. So when the doctor said, "you're doing all of that," she was amazed. She began to ask me what type of business I had. When she learned it was a kid spa, she wanted to hear more. When I shouted out the name of my company, almost all of the eight or nine medical attendants in the room had either been to my spot or heard about it. Now the doctor knew for sure that I wasn't crazy because I was wise enough to get their money. I was smart enough to hire a group of white kids and put them in the front after I experienced racism at the beginning of the business. It taught me to stay in the back and swipe the credit cards. The doctor was intrigued by me and began to replay what she just witnessed. She said to me, "These were doctors, nurses, psychologists, and social workers that were patronizing you? impressive." Yup! That was me! That's when I knew my strength was powerful. Only a few hours prior, they wanted to label me and tried to convince me I had lost my mind. The doctor now became my angel. When we began to talk, instead of being upset that she could not find a diagnosis, she was obliged to the fact that I honestly knew what was wrong with me. She was trying to make sense of how I was handling all these things and never cracked up. She began to realize and understand my strength, so she began to ask me how she could help. She went even further to say we have to go over your schedule, and we have to find out what you can eliminate because I want you to thrive. I'm looking at her, and I'm crying because, for the first time in six years, someone understood me. It was like a weight lifted off of my chest. Not even my husband understood what I was going through, but how could he? He didn't understand what he was going through. I was his strong wife trying to stay strong for him, but hurt myself in the interim.

I started to tell the doctor that the business made the money, so the business wasn't going anywhere. I added that my husband gets on my nerves, but I was going to keep him too. After all, he was a hard-working man, and his faithfulness to me was endless. My children are here to stay. I only had three classes before I got my bachelor's degree, so that wasn't going away. The only thing left was that stupid robotic job that I should've never worked. The doctor said she would be honored to write off on medical as long as I needed so that I could exhaust all of my time. She was curious to know why I never quit, and I told her because I'm not a quitter. I'm not built to quit. I'm a fighter, and before I quit, I will work that job. I would do my best because that's who I am. I emphasized to her that my name meant more to me. Putting a red mark up under my name did not represent who I was. When she finished my paperwork, she made me make her a promise to continue to follow my dreams. She stated that I was strong, and there's a blessing in all of this for me. She was the angel that gave me the first step to understanding from a human perspective. God's plan was bigger than I could ever imagine for my life. She helped me to understand that my mission was clear, and I had to stay focused in order to get back to the true me.

Psalm 139:14 New International Version (NIV)
14 I praise you because I am fearfully and wonderfully made; your works are wonderful. I know that full well.

JOB AFTER JOB

After everything that we've been through, we still stood firm, strong and united in our marriage. There were many days when I wanted to know why I was so committed. Yet, there was a conviction in me that would not allow me to leave. It was like I had to go through changes in order to reap the reward, but while I was going through these changes it was so disheartening. As women there is only one thing that we want and that is stability. Stability is a form of love. That was one thing that I lacked in my marriage. I kept praying and I kept asking God to show me, reveal to me why I could not feel the stability that I needed. Why can't I get this from my husband? I knew in the back of my mind that he was a hard worker. I didn't understand why every time he started a job he would quit as soon as one thing didn't go his way. Now, I'm an entrepreneur, so I do understand the frustrations of a job, but I also understand that you have to go through some stuff when you're working for someone. Although I might not be employed within a company, my employers are my clients. So sometimes I have to take slack from my employers (clients) to get the job done. I know at the end of the day I reap the harvest of a payment (income). That's the ultimate goal. So, I didn't understand why if one thing went wrong he would quit. Why did he not understand that I needed stability? This created a lot of frustration and arguments. I could not process why he would quit and he could not process why I was angry.

Over the years, I kept looking at the pattern. God kept revealing to me the dynamics of what was going on. If I did not sit still to understand what was taking place I would not be able to share my testimony and teach other women what mental health challenges some men go through. It doesn't matter whether they had been incarcerated or not. It truly depends on their background and how they grew up. In my instance, it was prison for with my husband. What this showed me was that any little thing that someone said to him was a trigger. It was a trigger because while incarcerated he was being told what to do and had to deal with it incessantly. There was no choice or option; there were only mandates. Now the flexibility of being able to quit a job without thinking about the repercussions was a privilege. He had an option, and he was in control. But not only was he in control of his life, he was also in control of mine. So, understand when you're in a marriage the things we do and the choices we make not only impact you, it also impacts your partner. Not to mention your family and children. Everyone is affected by the decision that one makes. So, as I started paying more attention, God was allowing me to become more conscious of what we were experiencing in our marriage life after prison. This revelation woke me up out of my depression and it became clearer to me every day thereafter.

Although it was hard to watch and hard to go through, I had to learn how to tell him not to quit his job. It became a constant conversation for him to say "What do you think?" It got to a point where I got so annoyed to where I didn't have an opinion anymore. It was very hard for me to not have an opinion because I'm very opinionated. God awakened me and started to minimize my opinion to allow my husband to see the impact of the choices that he made and how they affected his marriage and his wife. Also, he realized that I was no longer interested in giving my opinion. It made him sit down and strategize and think a little clearer while making a final decision. Now this didn't happen overnight. It was a process that had to take place before he was able to grasp and see what was happening. It took a lot of time for him to make responsible decisions on his own because he usually relied on my opinion. In a marriage we want that, but this is not your traditional marriage. So, I had to do some untraditional things to eliminate my opinion, so that he could grow into the man that he was destined to be. Man that became a great sacrifice. I had endured so much BS and all the instability that came along with it. I experienced many sleepless nights not knowing whether or not we were going to have an income tomorrow because he decided to quit yet another job due to someone saying something wrong or doing something that he didn't like. In the end, I stuck by him. I knew the core of my husband was greater. I knew that God did not bring us this far and endure so much to let us fall.

The core of our marriage was so strong that we would overcome this obstacle. The question was when. That was the hard part. God kept us. Each time he went to a job he started to stay longer. The things that I said to him in the past were starting to make sense to him. It started to resonate. I would talk to him and tell him that he couldn't look at the amount of money he was making, but at what works with the family in terms of the job. So let me tell you what that looks like. Even though a job may pay a lot of money we have to look at whether or not the job brings home more money with or without benefits. Also, you have to look at the job that pays little money but has all the benefits that you may need. These options must be considered when making employment decisions while providing for your family. So he had to learn and understand the process that it's not how much money you earn, it's what you do with the money once you earn it. Ponder on that for a minute. If a job offered a pension, health benefits and was $3 less than a job that paid more without benefits it was in my opinion a better fit to accommodate the needs of a family. You have to look at the future for both you and your family. Just like when you get older you have to consider your health. These are some of the things that I taught him to evaluate. So when I decided to pull away and allow his opinion to matter and not think about mines he was still able to hear my voice in his head. He was already taught to process the information and to strategize a plan that would benefit him and his family. You can accomplish anything that you pursue in life when you administer it strategically. By the time my husband was able to strategize and make responsible decisions it took years. It was years later when we overcame that hurdle. I'm glad that I stuck by him because one thing about women, our intuition is always on point. My husband is the last of a dying breed. He always said it and I always knew it. There will always be a sign within your relationship that will let you know whether or not to stay or leave. Now without judgment or without paying attention to judgment when people judge. What will you believe? How much is enough for you? I knew that there was something greater in my marriage and I knew that I had to stick it out to see. IT WAS WORTH IT!!!

DEATH IS NEVER EASY TO PROCESS

Life was good and we were taking life one day at a time. We finally found the peace we were looking for. My husband was working and a little more focused. However, the holidays were approaching, and I had a need to be around family. I talked to my husband and I let him know that I wanted to go to New Jersey to celebrate Thanksgiving with our families and he said OK... (he always tries to make me happy. It's the little things that makes me smile). He had to work until Thanksgiving Day, so he said he would meet us then. So as I always do, I made sure that my husband had dinner prepared, made sure his clothes were washed and packed (worry free). I wouldn't feel right if I didn't make sure he was straight before I left. Even though I was a retired hairstylist, I love dipping and dabbing in it. Every time I went to New Jersey I always had some of my old my client's setup for service. Smart huh... ain't nothing wrong with making a few extra dollars, I wasn't that damn depressed. I would have my work bag and I would be on the go as soon as I crossed those state lines. I loved catching up with my old clients and fellowshipping with them. Boy it was like old times. The twins were very faithful customers. Every time they heard I was coming to New Jersey, they would be the first to set up an appointment. I would go to their house and they would have more clients lined up for me to service. They kept me going, but in a good way. Before I knew it, I would have spent the whole day with them. This particular day when I got up there, I started to do one of the twins' hair and my husband called me in a panic. I immediately knew something bad had to happen because he never calls. I began to panic because he couldn't articulate what was wrong. I repeatedly yelled... what is it, please... tell me what is it? I listened to my husband cry. He's so strong and never shows his emotions. I asked him again what's wrong and he began to say:

"Tah, she's gone, she's gone."

"Who's gone," I yelled.

"My mother, she died."

I was in complete shock. I didn't know how to respond. I didn't know what to do for my husband being states away. I couldn't even embrace him in his time of sorrow. I did all that I knew to do which was to reach out to our church family for support in my absence. Just like that our deacon was there in a nanosecond. I was a little relieved that our deacon made it over there because someone needed to be with my husband during his time of sorrow. Most undeniably with depression and PTSD, he needed that support. As we were trying to figure out what was going on, I was really really bothered because I requested that his mother come spend Thanksgiving with us, yet her sister (caretaker) declined the offer. She stated that they were going to Atlanta to spend the holiday with her daughter. In my mind, you have to travel through the Carolinas to get to that destination. Respectfully, I

147

uttered those words to her because I didn't understand the issue. I commenced to say, let her stay with us while you go visit your daughter and she can visit with her son. But that didn't happen. I was even more hurt because now his mother is in an entirely different state and she dealt with panic attacks and that was what initiated her demise. What made that attack different from previous attacks was she also had a lingering cold (per the paramedics). They stated that her body had accumulated so much mucus in her throat which choked her to death, so much for the holiday. Thanksgiving would never be the same again.

Our 4-day visit turned out to be a two week stay. Get this, not only did we have to plan a funeral (so we thought), but we had to also plan for an additional cost to get the body back to NJ. This was too much to process. How many of y'all know that funerals and weddings can tear families apart? Most of you right? Well, if you didn't know it before, you do now, simply SICKENING! Keep reading because there's more to tell. My mother-in-law only had two children. My husband was the oldest. They were not able to plan their own mother's funeral or have a say in it. Of course, you know this was all about those mighty dollars, that's crazy right? They were only allowed to attend the funeral service. Here's the funny part, my family was all set to jump in and help, but once my husband's oldest aunt (matriarch of the family) took control, my family and friends fell back. Wouldn't you? I mean we tried to get insurance on her and that never happened (never allowed her to visit), our hands were tied. However, my

148

husband and his brother should have been privy to making their mother's arrangements. Come on, they're grown. The only time they were called upon was to ask how much money they could contribute. One thing about me, I do not play money games with ANYONE. All the money that my friends and I contributed was paid directly to the funeral home. No matter what I went through with my mother, one thing for certain, I knew she had my back. Moreover, she loves her son-n-law. My mother was ready to help us financially to make the funeral happen. But with all the negative energy my mother witnessed, she said she would be on the back end prepared to handle anything outstanding. My mother definitely was not going to allow anyone to control her finances. The apple doesn't fall far from the tree.

Once I realized how this was going with my husband's family, I began to think about my relationship with my mother-in-law. When we got together, I would get her to talk. Ironically, this was a huge deal because talking was not her thing. She was very quiet, but when she did talk, I would experience another side of her that was not often shown. We would enjoy our time together and I would always braid her hair into a ponytail and pin her hair-bun on the top of her head. She loved that style. If I wasn't able to do anything else in regards to the funeral, this was my only request, to be able to do her hair for her burial day.

I had to call and get permission from her older sister. The Matriarch is a different sister from the caregiver and she granted me permission to do her hair and purchase my mother-in-law's attire. That made me feel good during this time. I purchased my mother-in-law a beautiful navy blue suit and I went to the morgue of the funeral home and had my private moment with her. We usually would eat fried pork chops together, so I ate one before I did her hair. She had old braids in her hair that I had to cut out before I could even start. Once I got her hair loose, I washed her hair and greased her scalp. Then, I blew it dry as if she was awake. I embraced that time with my mother-n-law. My husband didn't even know I had it. All I could think about was is if I would have pushed my husband a little harder to get his mother, would she still be here today? Especially when I look at my daughter, she looks just like her.

Anyway, after my mother-n-law was dressed, I applied her lip gloss on her lips and put the lip gloss tube inside her inner jacket pocket. I whispered to my mother-n-law to make sure her lips were shining when she reached Heaven. She looked beautiful. I told her that I would make sure my husband would be ok and my brother-in-law too. I asked her to protect my husband because he had so much mental anguish added by her transition. I shared with her that life was heavy for him, but he will be ok and she could sleep in peace knowing I got him here on Earth. My husband couldn't even bring himself to view the body the day before the service or on the day of the service. It was a lot he had to process. He had to relive the fact that he was absent in his mom's life due to choices he made

150

on the streets. Every day was a reminder about his past. Some days were better than others. The sad part was his family was so consumed with judgment that they never took the time to see how the trauma of incarceration impacted his life after prison. I won't go into details about that situation, but this was something else that my husband had to go through with me by his side.

Your Honor, I don't know if the Ladies and Gentlemen of the jury understand what the lack of emotions looks like, but it is definitely triggered from being incarcerated. Life in prison prevents inmates from showing emotions. Showing emotions shows signs of weakness. Therefore, my husband didn't know how to truly grieve his mother's death; instead he carried the weight on his shoulders. His eyes would deliver a cold glare, but when I touched him or embraced him, I could feel his whole soul wanting to fall out. I was helpless as his wife because I didn't know how to stop his pain.

I knew mentally he was going through a lot, but my husband felt some kind of way the day of his mother's funeral. Even in the midst of him trying to mourn his mother, the female cousins were on their bullshit. Trying so hard to get under my skin but not caring how their actions would affect my husband at the same time. They were so disrespectful; they should have had a little more compassion for the aunt at least. Not only were they trying to disrespect me, but they also tried to disrespect our union by trying to divide us when they sat us down for the service. Trying to hold my tongue was hard. They sat my husband on the first row (in front of the body) and I sat in a chair behind my husband. All I could do is laugh on the inside because that was a true representation of our life. I always had his back. I held onto him, so that he knew I was near, but those cousins kept pushing. The disrespect got worse. It took everything in me to not lash out. They really had the nerve to bring his child's mother to the front where my husband was seated. I had to sit there and mentally process how this family truly did not respect our union. But how could they when they envied what we had. Despite the funeral, my husband recognized the buffoonery they tried. What they needed to know was that it didn't matter how hard they tried; we were solid. My husband is always on point, no matter how hard you try to live right, someone will always try you. The old me would have lashed out with aggression and rage. But my husband taught me how to be humbler. Even though I'm not all the way there yet. The best part of this was that neither of us gave in to the nonsense. We took the high road and my husband moved to the second row with me. We are two hearts that beat as one. I know y'all probably thinking oh! She was only their support. The support is fine but the way the support was delivered came across as some FUCKERY. Did I say that? My apologies...excuse my language. Stop being naive girl. Bullshit comes dressed up in all types of fashion. Supporting and needing to be seen are different. As a woman of God, you're supposed to move with grace. There is a time and place for everything, apparently, she didn't know this. I was neither threatened nor intimidated because the one thing that I was sure of 110%, was my husband's faithfulness, loyalty, and dedication for our family. There are so many other stories that I could go into, but this is a short story and I can't go into all those details. The funeral was crazy, but it went past us and we continued to soar. I kept fighting against the enemy. I realized that God strengthened me to overcome hatred. It was becoming clearer for me to understand that biting my tongue was not in vain. What I was experiencing was spiritual warfare to test my transformation God was in the process of doing. I needed to go through this because it had a purpose and I planned to walk in my purpose.

My husband lost his maternal grandmother while in prison and his paternal grandmother a few years after his release. He also lost a few uncles and aunts not far apart, that's a lot of death for a person that lost 10 years of their life behind the prison wall. But, once he returned to the streets, he realized the value of life and how fast life can dissolve right before your eyes. I couldn't begin to imagine what my husband was feeling on the inside of the coldness. Can you imagine how much more those deaths impacted his PTSD? What I did know was to have his back each and every time death occurred because I'm his ride or die[18]. I always made sure that I was strong enough for him. The thought of death now overwhelms me. After all that went on, I let my husband know that it was a big pill for

---

[18] Unconditional supporter

me to swallow and that I needed to go on a vacation to relieve my mind of all the stress, guilt and frustration that had taken over me. I didn't care about money, the bills, our families, or anything. Vacationing was my mental escape from life. For me, I could be dead broke, but go on vacation. Meditating on the white sand and seeing the bluish-green waters was how I found my peace. Check this out, let me show you how my mind expands when I free it from the world. When I cruise for example, as I dock waiting to set sail, I see an oversized ship sitting in water. However, the minute that ship embarks into the sea, I see God's greatness unfold right before my very eyes. The ocean has no end and the boat becomes a miniature piece of metal in the ocean God created. I'm able to process that God is able to do all things if you let Him. A mini vacation would allow me the chance to think of new strategies to get back where I needed to be. The thought of being on the water with no interruptions was all I needed to conjure up my next move. My husband needed that break too, so a seven-day cruise is what it was.

BROTHER –N-LAW

The funerals didn't stop. Shortly after burying my mother- in-law my husband received a phone call about another family member who died. Here we go again! We're trying to make arrangements to get back to New Jersey. Personally, I'm over funerals and my husband took this field trip alone. I'm not going to spend too much time talking about the burial because this chapter is to isolate how my husband lied to slowly move his brother into our home without discussion. So, here's how that looked. My husband did not call me when he left New Jersey. However, when he was almost in North Carolina, he called to tell me that his brother was coming to visit for a week. How many of you know that it wasn't just for a week? It turned into living in my space without warning. I was pissed! These are the things that broke down our line of communication. Someone visiting and someone staying are two different things, but both need prior conversation to discuss the terms and conditions of the stay and that conversation did not happen. These were the type of situations that made me feel violated and unconsidered especially when were trying to get on our feet. Once I realized that this was no longer a visit, I helped my brother-in-law find a job.

Now Ladies and Gentlemen of the jury let's pause right here for a second. Let me make myself clear, I am not saying that we shouldn't help others. But here is the reality:

1. It should be a conversation that happens (both parties' needs to be on the same page).

2. You should be in a position where you can help someone else where it is not hurting you (note: we were in the process of re-establishing our savings to move forward).

3. You can't help someone when someone is helping you (keep in mind my mother is helping us, so how can we be privy to help someone else).

Let me expound on that for a minute. We were living in my mother's rental property whereby she was not charging us market rent so that we could get our finances back in order to put us in a position to buy our own home. It was a slap in my mother's face to have my brother-in-law move into her home without her consent. Incarceration prevented my husband from thinking logically. When moving someone else into your home you must consider how you will be impacted economically. The utility bills increase and the cost of food goes up. Also, let's not forget that my mother is looking for extra money for rent. Go figure. I don't think this was something that my husband thought about. I don't think that he viewed the situation in that perspective. Instead, he viewed me as being the bad guy, or should I say selfish by refusing to help his brother. But that wasn't it. We have to look at the situation from every angle that's why a conversation should always take place. Once we realized that he was going to live with us, I had to discuss this with my mother. This was a side conversation that I needed to have and didn't know what it was going to do to my relationship with her. In spite of everything else, I still have to maintain a relationship with my mother outside of a business relationship while living in her rental property. At this point, it was imperative to help my brother-in-law to get a job. So once he secured the job, reality hit. My husband was going to work while my brother-in-law was in need of a ride to and from work. He had no license and no car. Suddenly, this situation became my responsibility. Damn, was I even considered! I felt bombarded, disrespected and violated. How could he do this? How could my husband do this to me? Why couldn't my husband consider what it would be like for an additional adult to be in our home? Why didn't he understand where I was coming from? Instead, I was looked upon as the enemy. The family started talking and everyone was pointing fingers at me. They all were on the outside looking in. But it didn't matter to me because I had thick skin. I really didn't care how anyone else felt. My only point to prove was to my husband. So that my husband could realize and understand that one person makes a difference. We had to be secure. We had to stabilize our life. For me, I already lost everything and sacrificed it all for my husband and his freedom. Now here I am in a mental prison not knowing how to escape. I didn't know how to get back to being me because I was placed in an inconsiderate situation. I was always trying to pull myself out of situations due to emotional decisions that were made without any form of communication. As for my mother, that relationship became sour. On the outside looking in, she was thinking there was extra money coming from somewhere. Who wouldn't think like that? I couldn't blame her. Unfortunately, I kept those conversations to myself to avoid more conflict. I was hurting, beat down and torn up. So, for me it was easier to be silent. But I wore my heart on my sleeve. So you can imagine the tension. It wasn't comfortable. How could it be?

At this time, I had an additional man in my home that I'm cooking for while my husband is at work. I never felt comfortable catering to a man other than my husband. Brother-in-law or no brother-in-law, a man is a man and as a woman I needed to feel comfortable in my own space. Maybe I would have felt differently if our finances were in order and we were moving in a positive direction in our own space within our own home. Nevertheless, that wasn't the situation. I felt like we were adding more baggage and we were falling deeper and deeper into a financial rut in which we didn't have to. So that's why this selfish decision was a problem for me. Do I love my brother-in-law? Yes, with all my heart! However, the Bible states that the man is a hunter and if I don't allow my husband to fall short, why would I standby and allow another man to fall short. Meditate on that for a minute.

2 Thessalonians 3:10, New International Version (NIV)
"For even when we were with you, we gave you this rule: 'The one who is unwilling to work shall not eat."

He didn't stay long and I thank God for where we are today in our relationship. I love him. Oh yeah, I love my husband too! Life is good. My brother-in-law lives on his own now and pays bills, so finally he can relate to where I was coming from. So, that's a good thing. Most importantly, it was a lesson learned from this situation.

MONEY, MOTHER & ME

So I guess you thought I was over talking to you about my mother's house. Not even. The tension was thick and even more intense between my mother and I because I needed my mother, (not the businesswoman), to understand my pain and depression. However, the business relationship always took precedence over the mother and daughter relationship. How do you think that made me feel? It was already hard enough to try and maintain a relationship or have the mother and daughter relationship that every girl dreams of. But mine was compromised. Here's why, in my mother's mind she had to make the mortgage and in my mind I wanted her to make the mortgage. Regardless, my mental health was being challenged. This was something my husband also had to learn. He would think I was just being lazy, but I just couldn't clear the cloud in my mind. Meanwhile, it was still a battle for my husband to understand how to pay bills. He would say "I am not going to be broke," and I would try to get him to see the difference. Being broke and having the bills unpaid is not the same as having no money and the bills met. That was a huge hurdle we had to overcome. Prioritizing bills matters. So this is all a part of the growing pains after prison. Keep in mind, they say the same amount of time that it takes to do prison time is the same amount of time it takes to undo the institutionalized mentality. That's a fact, I lived it. People would say "Oh he's over that" but they're on the outside looking in. I lived it firsthand. I can only be transparent and tell you my truth. There are still moments to this day that I may experience a behavior or two. As long as my husband continues to show progress, I will support him and be right by his side. Let me get back on track. My mother would send appraisers over while I was in the home. It was getting bad and I just wanted to walk away, but knew I was bigger than the obstacle and God was bigger than me. How do you think that made me feel? There's nothing like a woman feeling that she doesn't have stability. I'm not talking to you as if you don't know. All women desire two things: affection and stability. Men on the other hand like to feel needed and wanted. They think with their minds while women think with their emotions. Emotionally, I was very unbalanced. I was trying to fight all of these competing relationships: mother and daughter, husband and wife, brother-in-law and sister-in-law, stepson and stepmother, and son and daughter. Does it ever end? I was overwhelmed. I had to think about my mother selling the house from up under us and not knowing where our family was going to go. Although I was angry at the time, God allowed me to see it from a different lens. I was gaining my strength back without even knowing. All I had to do was talk to God and be detailed in my request. I was able to understand the business side of it. Now that is. So, I couldn't blame her at all, but then enough was enough. It was an eye opener for me. We had to get on top of our game and fast because our daughter depended on us. So much for the depression and everything else that was holding me back, I was not about to lose this game called life. CHECKMATE! God came through again!

TAKING OFF THE BLINDFOLD

Although the move was very abrupt, and we did not have time to prepare it was needed. It was needed because it motivated us to make it happen. I love for someone to make me feel as though I can't. For example, I had a long-term friend who always made herself available during the time I was going through my depression. She kept helping me and thought I needed her. She was handicapping me so that I could not surpass her but look how God works. When you talk to God, He will show you who people really are. I realized that she only helped me to keep me blindfolded. Eventually, God took the blindfolds off. In reality, God was showing me all along. I just needed to sit still to see him at his best. I thank God for my obedience.

I thank God for everything that we went through. Everything that we went through was a journey. I can see how my husband did ten years in prison. It took us a decade to go through trial and error for us to come to a common ground to understand what we both were going through and what we both needed. Once we identified that it was not stopping us. We stepped out on faith. We cleared our debt and cleared everything that we needed to do to get back to who we really were in God. I found myself and as for my husband, we had a plan. I was trying not to frustrate him and overwhelm him with bills because those things triggered his anxiety. This is why our method was: he works and I disperse the payments accordingly. I look at the bills and I know what needs to be done. I know how to prioritize the bills so that everything can move forward. We discussed the woman who ran off with our deposit money for the house in New Jersey. Here we were about to pay $250,000 for a house that was in the hood, beat up, and located on a street where a lot of violence and shootings took place. God said "Be patient, you need to understand what I have for you is greater than you can ever imagine," and by being patient and listening to God's word we were blessed immensely. As far as the move, God put us into a ranch home where the landlords were awesome. They helped us out, worked with us, showed us a little about investing, and enlightened us on a lot of things. God plants people into your life that are needed to elevate you and get you to the next step. Sometimes you don't know why those people are there until you actually experience it. Well, we experienced it and we experienced these great people that now became a part of our family.

God allowed us to clear our debt and improve our credit in a year. So let me backup for a minute. When my friend put us on her credit card it was about a few months before we had to move. We lived in that house and didn't know which way to go. So we didn't use the credit, it just sat there for almost a year. Then God started to show me the direction to come back to who I really am. The strong, confident, ambitious and outgoing person that I am known to be. God re-iterated these characteristics within me. I was able to pick up those credit reports up and comb through them because I already understood how credit worked. I needed my "FRIEND" to have us removed from that credit card. It wasn't helping us at all, so removing the credit card was a must. Improving our credit scores to get into a house of our own was a short-term goal. We were going to do it and no one could stand in our way. Let me enlighten you on this whole credit card situation so you're clear moving forward.

Let me give you a little background on the credit that the friend "was trying to help us" with. It was imperative that we have the charge removed from the credit report in order for us get a pre-approval. You see what she did was allowed it to look like it was good credit. So, on the credit report if you opened it up everything was green and everything was paid on time. But, here is where we got kicked in the back. She ran the credit card up and was only making minimum payments. Which means if the credit card was maxed out, it made us look like we had more debt. I was blind because I was going through depression. With all these different scenarios, uncertainties as well as the imbalance of my mental health, I didn't realize that it was actually an illusion of helping me improve my credit score. It allowed me to see the credit report and see that it was all good, everything is all green. Yes, we're going to get this house! However, in hindsight it wasn't helping us get the house. It was informing the creditors that I kept a lot of debt. Let me explain, the credit card was only $2,500. If I had a clear mind, I wouldn't have allowed someone to put a $2,500 credit card on my credit report in order for me to establish credit. I don't know what kind of friends you have, but I know within my circle of friends, we all wanted to help each other. We all go through a cycle in life where everyone goes through something or everyone needs someone.

When you honestly have someone's back you are there to help them get ahead. That is the way God set this lifestyle up. God set us up to reach back and help. If God helps you, who are you to not reach back and help someone else? So, we would put each other down on credit cards so if you fell short we helped you get back up so you wouldn't lose your credit ratings. Therefore, you would be put on a credit card with a substantial limit. For instance, a credit card with at least a $25,000 credit limit. I mean you're trying to prove you can handle debt. I know y'all probably thinking, "Are they sharing credit?" No, we were sharing credit numbers and ratings not actual credit cards. We only needed to show consistent payments on our credit report to boost our credit rating to help rebuild or establish credit. We're not using the credit card(s), that's not the goal. The goal was to show the creditors that we were reducing our debt. However, this was not what my so-called friend did for us. Due to having blindfolds on, I didn't see it until God showed me and everything made sense. It also made sense not to be bitter towards her. I love her and will always have a place in my heart for her. Will I ever trust her again? NEVER! We will never be the way we used to be, EVER! You know the old saying "ONCE A TIGER SHOWS YOU

THEIR TRUE SPOTS BELIEVE THEM." I won't say that I won't ever speak to her again, but for me, it can only be cordial. Sometimes you outgrow people, places and things, remember that. Life will take you places where everyone can't go with you. They are there with you for a season, reason, or a lifetime. It is up to you to understand who falls under which category. In this situation, she was there for a REASON, but she was definitely not in my life for a lifetime.

Consequently, I thank God for allowing me to gain consciousness and understanding. I can walk back into the true me and shine bright. Ladies and Gentlemen of the jury tell your friends to "KEEP THEIR SHADES ON" because you can also shine bright. All you have to do is stay focused and determined. You can do anything and everything through Christ. I play the game of chess in life. I move quietly so that people do not know what my next move will be and that's exactly what I did. The so-called friend who put us on her credit was not doing anything to move forward. She assumed that we wouldn't have anything. She assumed that we were stuck. It took us a year to sign our documents for a house. Not just any house but a brand-new house that we built from the ground up in an affluent neighborhood.

GOD HAD TO BREAK ME DOWN
TO BUILD ME BACK UP...

AND HE BUILT US A HOUSE TOO!

While she thought that we were not moving at all, we were moving at a fast pace. We were moving at a pace so fast that no one could stop us. Did you hear me? A BRAND NEW HOUSE from the ground up. We paid the same amount of money or maybe less than we would have been paying in the hood. As my mother would say, "You're like the Jeffersons, moved on up to the eastside!" It sounds so good and feels good too. God blessed us and a year later we had our house keys and walked through our front door! When we stayed focused on the plan, not allowing anyone or anything to interfere in our lives and worked as a team, God showed us that the way we started the process was the way we were supposed to finish it.

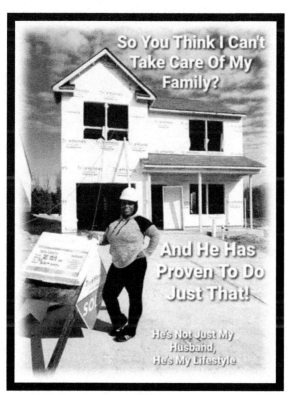

I thank God that we were able to see that and understand our strengths. Some people may view things and think that "he (my husband) is not being a man." My pastor would say, "He is being more than a man, because a man's job is to understand his strengths. "Paying the bills was not his strength. His strength was going to work and allowing me who understood finances to manage the bills. As you can see the success followed. I thank my husband for being a man who understands how well we work as a team. It's not about what people think, because people will talk. Does it matter? It only matters if you allow it to penetrate.

God is going to take you through some things and those things are only meant to strengthen you, to show and prove that you will overcome and you will surpass everything that people doubted. But if you keep moving forward, God will allow the light to shine on you so bright, on the man that you choose to be with or the man that chooses to be with you and who is truly down for you. People will never understand what happened. When I tell my story it is very simplified, believe me. The only thing that I can say is that it was no one but God who blessed me (US). Try it for yourself, I did.

HOME SWEET HOME!

TEAM WORK ALWAYS MAKES
THE DREAM WORK

Romans 15:5 New International Version (NIV)
5 May the God who gives endurance and encouragement give you the same attitude of mind toward each other that Christ Jesus had,

CLOSING ARGUMENT TO THE COURT

To date, I have been married to my husband, that former prisoner, yes, that now felon, for a little over a DOZEN of years since his release. I can't share with you enough that GOD is not only REAL but, my my my, he is a working God. Although I may NOT be a licensed therapist, I have something that has more value, experience. Having the necessary experience under my belt makes me the most qualified to deliver therapy to other's mental health. There is power in Preservation and Community in Education. In closing, let me reassure you...you are not alone; so, let's walk this journey together. Your Honor, thank you for allowing me this moment to testify. To the Jury and the People of the Court, I don't know if I have said enough to persuade you to free me, but I know this battle is not mine, but the Lord's. For that, I have peace either way it goes.

Judge: Has the jury reached a verdict?

Jury: We have your Honor. We the jury find the defendant Totisha Phelps-

- Guilty by association to the 1st degree
- Guilty of falling in love, and
- Guilty of resisting self-care and self-love

Judge: You have heard the defendant's testimony and the jury's verdict. It is now time for sentencing. Totisha, may you please stand. You have been found

INNOCENT in the eyes of the Lord and are sentenced to:

- The rest of your lifetime loving you first
- Helping other women like you to overcome
- To sharing your story with the world because they need to hear it!

"COURT IS NOW ADJOURNED!"

IT'S OK TO BE SELFISH

The moral of the story is this, being in love can sometimes sidetrack your mind and you slowly drift away from who you really are. We have to consciously make a decision to stay in tune with ourselves and set limitations and boundaries for the people whom we love. This may mean learning to say NO or NOT RIGHT NOW. Not only say it but say it with authority and be comfortable when saying it. Ladies and Gentlemen of the jury, we have to keep our mind, body, and spirit in alignment to work as one in pursuit of our best. If we are no good for ourselves, we cannot be a sound mind for anybody else (spouse, lover, kids, family, work, church, etc...). Find you a space, place, or activity that brings you peace from the world. I am not sure where you are spiritually, but I know everyone in this court room can relate. When cruising, I am able to see God's work in 3D. I mean, God divided the waters from the sky and separated the light from the darkness. He created the mammals of the sea, the birds that fly over me and male from female. That's when I remember, he also created me. So, who am I to minimize God's creation? Sometimes you have to be selfish in order to get yourself together (never feel guilty for it either). You have to make you matter first. Being selfish is healthy if done with the only intention of gaining self-preservation because the reality is this, people will deplete you for their selfish needs if you let them.

Genesis 1: New International Version (NIV)
1 In the beginning God created the heavens and the earth.

FINAL THOUGHT

Although my husband was the subject of the story, the story was not just about him. To be mentally locked up is worse than being locked physically. It is my prayer you received my transparency and was able to identify with me. Guess what? You teach people how to love and treat you, when you learn how to love you first. Self-Love is the Best Love. However, GOD'S LOVE is the GREATEST LOVE of them all!!

"I'M BLESSED, GOD HELD ONTO ME WHILE I WAS HOLDING ONTO HIM!"

Psalm 139:14 New International Version (NIV)
14 I praise you because I am fearfully and wonderfully made; your works are wonderful, I know that full well.

THE HEALING BEGINS WITH YOU

When I would start to feel alone, I would write down my feelings. This became my escape room, my therapy and above all, my peace without any interruption or judgment. I cannot begin to tell you how much POWER is in a PEN and a simple piece of PAPER. This was my form of meditation and the key to my tranquility. I adopted this approach because it allowed me to void out everything and everyone around me, it became my outlet to begin to HEAL. Words cannot describe how light I felt after I told someone off without having to compromise or listen to their rebuttal. Can you imagine that? All you have to do is, write, that's it, just write. I thought you wouldn't believe me! So I have taken the liberty to get you started. The next few pages are for you to release your feelings by telling that one person that is getting on your everlasting nerves right now... (We all have one) how they made you feel. Make them understand how they make you feel and you will feel free. You don't have to believe me. However, I challenge you to try it for yourself, *PICK UP THE PEN and WRIIIIIITE.* Oh! I forgot to tell you, don't send it, this is about your HEALING, your PEACE and your SERENITY!

GOD,
grant me the
Serenity
to accept the things
I cannot CHANGE;
Courage
to CHANGE
the things I can;
and
Wisdom
to know the DIFFERENCE.

(My husband's Daily Prayer of Comfort)

THE WORK STARTS HERE
"Journal Today & Unlock Your Feelings Tomorrow"

THE WORK STARTS HERE
"Journal Today & Unlock Your Feelings Tomorrow"

THE WORK STARTS HERE
"Journal Today & Unlock Your Feelings Tomorrow"

THE WORK STARTS HERE
"Journal Today & Unlock Your Feelings Tomorrow"

THE WORK STARTS HERE
"Journal Today & Unlock Your Feelings Tomorrow"

THE WORK STARTS HERE
"Journal Today & Unlock Your Feelings Tomorrow"

THE WORK STARTS HERE
"Journal Today & Unlock Your Feelings Tomorrow"

THE WORK STARTS HERE
"Journal Today & Unlock Your Feelings Tomorrow"

THE WORK STARTS HERE
"Journal Today & Unlock Your Feelings Tomorrow"

THE WORK STARTS HERE
"Journal Today & Unlock Your Feelings Tomorrow"

THE WORK STARTS HERE
"Journal Today & Unlock Your Feelings Tomorrow"

THE WORK STARTS HERE
"Journal Today & Unlock Your Feelings Tomorrow"

THE WORK STARTS HERE
"Journal Today & Unlock Your Feelings Tomorrow"

THE WORK STARTS HERE
"Journal Today & Unlock Your Feelings Tomorrow"

THE WORK STARTS HERE
"Journal Today & Unlock Your Feelings Tomorrow"

THE WORK STARTS HERE
"Journal Today & Unlock Your Feelings Tomorrow"

THE WORK STARTS HERE
"Journal Today & Unlock Your Feelings Tomorrow"

THE WORK STARTS HERE
"Journal Today & Unlock Your Feelings Tomorrow"

THE WORK STARTS HERE
"Journal Today & Unlock Your Feelings Tomorrow"

THE WORK STARTS HERE
"Journal Today & Unlock Your Feelings Tomorrow"

THE WORK STARTS HERE
"Journal Today & Unlock Your Feelings Tomorrow"

THE WORK STARTS HERE
"Journal Today & Unlock Your Feelings Tomorrow"

Stay Connected

INSTAGRAM: @LNKPWA

FACEBOOK: @LNKPWA

TWITTER: @LNKPWA

WEBSITE: www. Locknkeypwa.com

EMAIL: Locknkeypwa@outlook.com

Available for Hire, i.e., Coaching, Workshops, Public Speaking Engagements, and More!!

ABOUT THE AUTHOR

Totisha L. Phelps, was born and raised in Newark, NJ but relocated to North Carolina in 2010. She is a CHARISMATIC yet BOLD, educator and motivator that loves to inspire people. As a child of God, wife, and mother, she is a pillar in her community who loves to travel, fellowship, and create memories that will last a lifetime.

She has a strong understanding that helping and serving others is the gift that keeps on giving. In her own words, "It is me, more than what you thought and all of what you see. I am me. BLESSED and HIGHLY favored! Thank you for your LOVE and SUPPORT"

Printed in Great Britain
by Amazon